I0656908

Theodore Russell Monro

County Versus Counter

A novel. Part 2

Theodore Russell Monro

County Versus Counter
A novel. Part 2

ISBN/EAN: 9783337048525

Printed in Europe, USA, Canada, Australia, Japan

Cover: Foto ©Andreas Hilbeck / pixelio.de

More available books at **www.hansebooks.com**

COUNTY VERSUS COUNTER

A Novel.

BY

THEODORE RUSSELL MONRO

AUTHOR OF

THE VANDELEURS OF RED TOR," "LOVE LOST, BUT HONOUR WON,"
ETC., ETC.

IN THREE VOLUMES.
VOL. II.

LONDON:
CHAPMAN & HALL, 193, PICCADILLY.
1878.

[All Rights Reserved.]

CONTENTS OF VOL. II.

CONTENTS.

———∞⋛∞⋛∞———

CHAPTER I.

A NEST OF HORNETS.

I N a little house in a dull street in Pimlico, two ladies sat at supper towards the end of June. They had been to the theatre. The heat had been overpowering, and the play rather dull; altogether both of them seemed in a dispirited condition.

There was champagne on the table, and seltzer and soda water. There was a cold fowl too, and a delicious salad; but neither of the ladies seemed to have sufficient energy even to draw a cork, much less to carve a fowl.

There was a third place laid at table; evidently some one else was expected, for whom these two were waiting.

The elder of the two ladies was a little woman, plump, without being fat, with small features and expressive grey eyes. Her age appeared to be about thirty, but she looked young at night, and old in the morning; old at any rate until her toilette for the day had been brought to a satisfactory conclusion, so that it was difficult to tell her age. This lady called herself Mrs. Astor.

The younger woman was her sister, but extremely unlike her. She was a tall, lithe, handsome brunette, a woman with pronounced features, which in a few years would make her look hard and stern, but which now were very handsome in a masculine style of beauty. Her eyes were very dark and large, the lower part of her face rather heavy, but powerful and expressive. Handsome she undoubtedly was, but hers was not a pleasant face to look upon. It was cold, and set, and cruel. The lips were very thin, and there was a curl in them whenever she spoke, which gave her a sneering and contemptuous look that was very far from agreeable to the majority of those who knew her. She did not appear to be more than eight and twenty, though she certainly was not less. Her name was Lizzy Mullins.

In all probability her godfathers and godmothers, if she had ever had any, had given her the name of Elizabeth or Eliza; but if so, it had never been made use of in her remembrance or her sister's. As far back as her memory would serve her, she had been Lizzy Mullins.

The appearance of these two ladies was a

great contrast to their surroundings. The little back parlour in which supper had been laid was grimy, and almost squalid in its appearance ; the tablecloth was not clean, the forks and spoons were of dull metal, the willow-pattern plates were chipped all over, while the once gaudy mirror over the chimney-piece was cracked from end to end.

The ladies' dress, on the contrary, was gorgeous in the extreme ; much more so than is at all usual with English women at the theatre ; while both of them were loaded with a profusion of jewels which the poverty of their surroundings stamped at once as "Brummagem."

Mrs. Astor wore a dress of pale pink satin, fitting very tightly to her plump little figure. Her neck and shoulders were bare, while she had but just laid aside a pair of pink gloves which reached almost to her dimpled elbows.

In her light brown hair, which was sprinkled with gold dust, she wore a paste diamond star and a small spray of pink heather, where her hair was gathered up in a knot at the back of her shapely little head.

Miss Mullins looked superb in white silk, trimmed with gold oak-leaves and acorns, wherever such could be placed; she wore them in her hair, at her breast, as shoulder-knots, and round the skirt of her dress, and her large white arms were covered with bangles, and her neck with a cascade of gleaming glass.

Both sisters were delicately tinted : Mrs. Astor pink, Miss Mullins a creamy white; but the heat of the theatre had told on their complexions, and the result was somewhat streaky and forlorn.

" Liz," said the elder sister suddenly, " I can't stand this sort of life much longer. It is weary, weary work, and we shall do no good in 'the little village;' suppose we try elsewhere?"

"Where on earth are we to go?" said Liz; "and where is the money to be found?"

Mrs. Astor sighed. "Give me the champagne," she said; "perhaps I shall find an idea when I am less weary. We have come to the end of our tether, my dear, and it will have to be 'neck or nothing.'"

She drank off a tumbler of champagne, and passed the bottle to her sister, who refreshed herself in like manner.

"Whatever happens we must make ourselves scarce out of this," said Mrs. Astor. "Duns are becoming too importunate, and the old woman here is beginning to smell a rat."

"Let her smell," said Liz; "she can find out nothing. She must have known we were hard-up, or we should never have come to this beggarly hole; as long as we can pay her her rent, I don't see what she can say."

" Has young Darell said anything more? You ought to have been able to make him propose to you by this time."

" He's not such a fool. These young London men are too wide-awake for that; one must find a green country bumpkin for that sort of dodge."

" How much money have you left from the last breach of promise case, Liz ?"

" Barely thirty pounds. Fancy only landing three hundred after all that fuss and bother !"

" It might have been worse," said Mrs. Astor. " He might have preferred to marry you rather than part with his money. He was a close-fisted old skinflint."

" I think I could have kept out of that trouble," said Liz, laughing. " He would have been glad to be quit of me at double the damages."

" I think the jury would have given you more, my dear, had it been your first public disappointment. Let me see, what did you get from young Jenkyns ?"

" Only a thousand," said Liz. " I ought to have had two at least."

" And from young Hopkins ?"

" You forget that never came before the court," said Liz. " His father gave me five hundred to hold my tongue, and let the young fool marry his cousin."

" Ah ! so he did. I had forgotten," said Mrs. Astor dreamily. " Well, we must fish in other waters. Only I do so hate being exiled from London. I would try Paris, only I can't speak a word of French."

" What sort of fish do you want, Anne ?"

" Breaches of promise won't do for me ; I could never go into court after all the scandal there has been. I suppose I shall have to get married again! Ugh!" and Mrs. Astor actually shuddered at the idea of matrimony.

"Well, I must admit you had a bad time of it, Anne. However, you have gained your experience; of course you will never make such a goose of yourself again."

"I don't know that. What other course is open to me? As I said before, breaches of promise are worthless to me now; as a *divorcée* no jury would give me a farthing, and I should have to pay costs for the amusement of hearing the man's letters read in public. No! I shall have to marry again; but I'll take care to choose better than I did last time, and I'll have a sum of money down before the ring is on, on my next matrimonial journey."

"Ah! if you did that, you might slip the noose and keep the money."

"My dear Liz, I am getting old and faded;

I don't mean to tempt fortune too far. If I can get a good offer, I shall take it, provided the man is one I can manage and I have a good settlement. It is not the state of marriage that is objectionable to me as it is to you. It was the husband fate had mated me with. Heavens! how I did loathe that man!"

"Where is he now?"

"I am sure I don't know, and don't care; I only hope he may never cross my path again."

"Still you can't say you treated him well, can you?"

"He treated me worse than I treated him; but I never put detectives on him as he did on me. If I had, he would never have been able to get his divorce, that I'll swear."

"It is a pity that other one died! Do you think he would have married you?"

" Married me ! Of course he would. He was one of the best and kindest fellows in creation, and he was only waiting for the decree *nisi* to be made absolute to make me his wife ;" Mrs. Astor laid her head on her hands and burst into a flood of tears.

" That's just the worst of you, Anne," said her sister in a hard tone. " You always will show up soft just at the wrong time. If you had no heart at all, like me, you would be ten times happier than you are. Here, have another glass of ' fiz.' The man is dead, and there's an end of it."

" But I loved the man !" gasped Anne hysterically. " Oh ! my God ! what a wretched woman I am !"

The younger woman gazed at the elder with a look of contemptuous annoyance.

" Come, Anne," she said, " this is no time for crying over spilt milk. It's a pity he died so suddenly. Otherwise he might have

done something for you at any rate.   As it
is, you must do something for yourself.   We
want our wits about us.   Tears ruin the
brain for prompt action.   Here, drink
this !"

Mrs. Astor drained another tumbler of
champagne.   Then she got up and wiped her
eyes, and smoothed her hair in the cracked
mirror over the fireplace.

There was a knock at the street-door ; a
knock from a man's hand, not from the
knocker.   It was repeated three times at
intervals.

" That is Con," said Liz, " pull yourself
together, Anne.   Don't let him see that you
have been crying."

Then she went to the door and opened it,
her silk skirts rustling as she went.

She delayed a minute in the hall to give
her sister time to efface the traces of recent
tears, told the visitor that Anne was not very

well. "The theatre had been so hot, and Anne always felt the gas."

Then she threw open the door, and Mr. Conrad Norton entered.

CHAPTER II.

HE was a slight, dark, handsome fellow of about thirty. His figure was symmetrical, and not lacking in either grace or power. He wore his hair very short indeed, and parted in the middle over a remarkably low but good forehead. His chin was clean-shaven, and he wore a heavy black moustache, a good deal curled up at the ends. His complexion was a dead white, more from the thickness of the skin than from lack of health; and his eyes were large and clear and lustrous, in colour almost black. His voice was low-pitched, and singularly pleasant in tone; while his manner was almost caressing, without being familiar, and possessed a nameless, indefinable charm, which few women could resist.

He was in evening-dress; the cut of his clothes was perfect, and he wore no jewellery of any sort; on his well-shaped hand was no ring. Altogether he seemed manly, unaffected, and well bred.

"Why did you not come to the theatre to-night?" asked Mrs. Astor, as she half rose to receive him. "We did not give you up till quite the end of the play."

"I was fortunate in making a new acquaintance at the club," answered Mr. Norton, "whose society was so pleasant that I could not tear myself away."

"So pleasant or so lucrative?" asked Miss Mullins.

"The terms are synonymous," said he. "My young friend had money which he seemed bent on losing, and I preferred to see him through the process of being plucked before he fell into other hands."

"Can you give him a name?" asked Liz.

"His name is Darell—Augustus Darell; as empty-headed a young coxcomb as I have met with for many a long day."

Miss Mullins looked at her sister. She paused a moment, then she said:

"I have a Darell on hand too; but he cannot be the same as this one. My young friend is uncommonly wide-awake; and, besides, his name is Adolphus, for I have heard him called 'Dolly' often."

"Dolly Darell!" exclaimed Norton, with a laugh; "you won't get much out of him. Dolly is a man who has bought experience, and I am proud to say he bought it of me several years ago. He has learnt wisdom since then. I should say there is hardly a 'cuter blade in the ' little village ' than Dolly Darell !"

" Your pigeon may be his brother," suggested Mrs. Astor.

" May be ; but it is hardly likely. There must be eight years' difference at least between the men ; and Dolly got warmed too much himself when he first came to town, for him to have let this young cub loose in London by himself. I rather hope they are not brothers, for my name was not Norton when I met Dolly Darell."

Then these three worthies supped, and put down a considerable amount of champagne, especially Mrs. Astor.

They seemed to be on very intimate terms, these three ; and yet there was certainly no flirtation, and no love. They had been useful to one another before, and it was pro-

bable they would be so again. Just now,
however, the question was how the ladies
were to live.

They were women with plenty of brains and
some accomplishments, the daughters of a
stock-broker who had failed and died, leaving
these two girls entirely alone in the world,
and with nothing to live upon. In the first
bewilderment of their grief and destitution,
an elderly man, who had known them from
childhood, and who wanted a wife, had
offered them both a home if Anne would
marry him. They were fast girls, not well
educated, and quite incapable of making a
livelihood as governesses, or, indeed, in any
respectable manner. Still, they had no intention of being other than respectable; and,
much against her will, Anne, who was
desperately in love with a penniless young
clerk in the city, at last consented to marry
the old gentleman, who was himself a

broker. He was bad-tempered, dirty in his habits, and repulsive in appearance.

The young wife endured him for two years. Then the old love turned up again, handsomer, fonder, more fascinating than ever ; and driven almost mad by her husband's coldness and neglect, she had listened, and had fallen.

The husband had become suspicious, and had employed detectives to watch her. Her infidelity had been proved beyond all doubt, and her husband had turned her into the streets. She had gone to the man who had been her ruin, and her sister had for a short time become companion to a girl of weak intellect, who was living at Folkestone. Then the man had died suddenly without marrying Anne ; while Liz had inveigled her charge's brother into a promise of marriage, which his family had been glad to nullify by the surrender of five hundred pounds.

The two sisters had lived on this for a time, and Liz, being entirely without scruples, and finding breaches of promise lucrative, had since landed two more men and mulcted them, one in a thousand and the other in three hundred pounds.

During the first two years Anne had given Liz a home; during the last three Liz had returned the compliment. But now at last they had come to the end of the younger sister's earnings, and some new means of livelihood must be found.

There was no need for reticence with Mr. Conrad Norton. He knew their whole history, had known Anne's husband and Anne's lover, and having provided Liz Mullins with her last victim, had pocketed a third of the winnings.

Mr. Augustus Darell had parted with one hundred and fifty pounds during his short acquaintance with Mr. Conrad Norton, and the latter gentleman was quite ready to assist the needy sisters in their hour of adversity. He listened to the story of their troubles with well-bred concern.

"As to duns," he said, " of course, paying any of them is preposterous. Get what you can in the course of to-morrow from all the tradespeople who can be induced to trust you, and have a telegram sent you to a dying relative about nine in the evening of to-morrow. Spoil the Egyptians to the utmost, and meet me at Blagden's Hotel in Church Street to-morrow night. We can all put up there for a night or two, while we plan a summer tour in the provinces. I have a plan in my head, but it requires reflection and development."

Then he departed, and lighting a cigar, strolled home thoughtfully to bed.

CHAPTER III.

ON the following day, Conrad Norton took rooms for himself, Mrs. Astor and her sister, at Blagden's Hotel, in Church Street. He said the ladies would arrive about ten o'clock in the evening, and he ordered a *recherché* supper, with cutlets, mayonnaise, lobster-salad, and champagne. He then went out to "spoil the Egyptians," as he termed it; he proceeded to order boots and shoes, clothes and linen, and even succeeded in obtaining a silver-mounted dress-ing-case from one credulous tradesman into whose shop he had once or twice been with a notorious nobleman whose acquaintance he had made abroad.   He was careful to avoid shops in much frequented thoroughfares. He wanted Bond Street and Piccadilly for lounging purposes; so Bond Street and Piccadilly were spared by Conrad Norton.

About eight o'clock he sent an urgent telegram to Mrs. Astor:

" Your sister dangerously ill.   Come instantly, and bring Eliza.   Had better throw up your lodgings.   Do not delay."

This telegram Mrs. Astor, apparently in the wildest state of alarm and grief, showed to the landlady.   Everything was ready beforehand, and " the spoils" obtained in the afternoon had not been unpacked; so, after some pretence at haste in the bedroom, and payment of their trifle of rent, Mrs. Astor and Miss Mullins got into a cab, and were seen in Pimlico no more.

Soon after their arrival at Blagden's Hotel, Mr. Norton joined them, and they proceeded, with the aid of lobster-salad and champagne, to discuss their future plans.

"It has quite recently come to my knowledge," said Norton, "that an old friend of mine has succeeded in catching a real earl, and has married him. I have often heard of the nobleman in question, though we have never met, and I believe he is a weak sort of idiot, who drank away what little brains he had long ago. I feel sure the countess will not refuse to consider my claims, as an old friend of hers before her marriage ; and, if once I can make good my own footing in that neighbourhood, I can, of course, smooth the way for you. The nobleman I speak of is Lord Margate ; his place is Coddesley, about a mile out of a deadly-lively little country town in Sandshire, called Olton Priors. The place is doubtless dull, but I think, when you have heard me out, you will say that a dull place is the best for our purpose. The townspeople are greener than spring onions, and there is a little furnished house to be let, by the year, in Olton Priors itself, which you two might take, and, of course, never pay for, unless with other people's money."

"How did you find out all this, Con?' said Mrs. Astor. "I don't think Sandshire will do at all. One might as well go to Stornoway, or the Hebrides."

"Wait till you have heard me out, my dear madam. You know I am very fond of a bout with the gloves. It keeps one's hand in for real fighting, and, in my vagabond sort of life, a knowledge of the 'noble art' is of great importance. Well, I looked in at the 'Owl and Dragon' the other day, and had a

few rounds with Bill Nash, the Roehampton
Pet ; and, while I was there, a chap came in
whom Bill knew something of, and to whom
he was giving lessons in the ' noble art.'
When we had both had our fill of Nash's
punishment, we had a round together, and
this made us rather chums. We talked a
good deal about the wrestling at Lillie
Bridge and the Welsh Harp, and so on ;
and he told me about some famous wrestling
matches which took place at Moreton Basset,
in Sandshire, about a month ago, in which a
friend of his, one Victor Ross, had borne off
the prize against all-comers. Then I found
Moreton Basset was not far from Olton
Priors, a place I have some interest in on
many accounts ; and when I asked him about
the neighbourhood, and the people who lived
in it, I found he knew something about
everybody there, being himself the son of the
landlord of the principal hotel in the place.

" What is the man's name ?" asked Liz.
" Is he likely to be useful ?"

" His name is George Warre, and he is
not likely to be useful in the way you mean,
Liz; but I mean to make him of great use
in furthering some little plans of my own.   I
have shown him about the 'little village,'
and put him up to a thing or two he didn't
know before, and, in short, been very civil to
the fellow. In return for my civilities, I
mean to stay at that hotel of his, in Olton
Priors, for a month or two this summer, and
to renew my acquaintance with my Lady
Margate ; and I thought the little furnished
house might be a pleasant summer retreat, in
which you could besport yourselves till fortune favours you."

" I don't see that your going to this man's
hotel will give us any opening in life," said
Liz, in a discontented tone.

" Wait a bit," answered Norton.   " This

fellow, Warre, is very confidential, and has
given me a sketch of the leading families in
that part of the world. You remember
Broom, the counter-jumper, who made a
fortune in tallow, or railway-grease, or something of that sort? At any rate, you
remember the name? Well, this Broom has
built a great stucco mansion on one bank of
the Shale, near Olton Priors, and has called
it—appropriately enough, by the way—
Buncombe. This man has a son, called
Plantagenet, who is very proud of the
descent the Herald's office found for his
father, from the house of Anjou. This
amiable youth is of a very amorous tem-
perament, and his heart is as yet free. If
one of you can't come round this soft young
Crœsus, it will be your own faults. If you,
Anne, really intend matrimony, from all I
hear you can't feather your nest better than
by going in for the ring."

" But the man has a father, you said, Con. Fathers are averse to a *divorcée* for an only son with money."

" Why should they know anything about the divorce?" said Con. "You may as well be hung for a sheep as a lamb. If you go down to Olton Priors at all, go as a widow — husband died in Australia ten months ago — desirous of retirement in a rural district. After the first month go into half mourning, after the first three, marry this young spark if you can, and make him pay for getting rid of you, if you can't."

" The last is more in Liz's way than mine. And what shall you want for the introduction, Con, and the light of your countenance throughout the campaign? Now that we are on the subject, we may as well have it all in black and white."

" If it is another breach of promise case, I shall want a third of the profits. If a marriage, a thousand pounds down six months after the knot is tied."

"The idea promises sport at any rate," said Liz, "and the furnished house seems ready to hand."

"We might shoot at a pigeon and hit a crow," said Mrs. Astor. "If we were sure we should get into good society, I think it would be worth the trial. There must be plenty of other men besides the Broom sprig."

"Lady Margate leads society down there," urged Con Norton. "I do not think she will refuse to call on you, if I ask her to do so."

There was a sneer on the young man's face as he said this, which was not lost on the sisters; a sneer which marred the beauty of his face, and made his expression that of a devil incarnate.

"To whom does this house you speak of belong ?" asked Mrs. Astor.

" To an old lady of the name of Trevor— Miss Priscilla Trevor.   Of course if you are her tenants, she will feel bound to take some notice of you.   You know better how to get round an old maid than I can tell you.   She knows everybody in the place, and for miles round, while the very fact of your being in a house of hers will give you an air of re- spectability, and make the tradespeople wait for their money until you are married to somebody or—or clear of the place."

" Suppose we were to meet some one who knew us !" said Liz.

" Well, suppose you do !   Come back to town by the next train, and I will do the same.   We shall at least have had some months of existence at other people's expense, and if we can't amuse ourselves as well, I think it will be our own fault.   Come, will you go ?"

" I'm all there," said Liz, laughing.   " If
Anne likes it, I will go."

" There is no choice," said Anne, " at least
I can think of nothing better."

' " Very well then, let us go," said Norton.
" Now you girls go to bed, and I will write
to Warre to take the furnished house."

CHAPTER IV.

THE HORNETS SETTLE.

IT was immediately on Warre's return to Olton Priors, that Conrad Norton's letter reached him at the Trevor Arms. It was a day or two after Miss Priscilla's garden-party, but yet in the last days of June.

Victor Ross had looked in at the Trevor Arms to see Warre, on his way from Black Rock to his timber-yard; and Warre showed him Norton's letter and told him in glowing terms of the new friend he had made in London.

" A regular slap-up swell, and no mistake," said Warre, speaking of Norton. " Thorough bred every inch of him ; and can't he handle his mauleys, that's all !   A clean-built, smart young chap, and as handsome as paint ! Now read his letter."

Victor read as follows :

" BLAGDEN'S HOTEL,
" CHURCH STREET, W.
" *June 28th.*

" MY DEAR WARRE,

" I have found Miss Trevor a tenant for the summer months, or by the year, if Miss Trevor prefers that arrangement.

" A very old friend of mine, a Mrs. Astor, who has recently been left a widow, desires to find some secluded spot in which to recover the first great shock of her irreparable loss.

" She will be accompanied by her sister, a young lady who has created a great sensation in London by her beauty; but they would prefer that you should find a couple of servants, a housemaid and a cook, who would be able to enter upon their duties at once, should Miss Trevor accept my friends as tenants.

" Mrs. Astor will be willing to meet any wishes Miss Trevor may express as to terms, as long as they are within reason. Money is no object to Mrs. Astor, her husband's death having left her in very affluent circumstances.

" If Miss Trevor agrees, telegraph to me here. Mrs. Astor is in delicate health, and needs immediate change of air.

" I think of coming down with them to see them comfortably into their new quarters, and if you will keep a room for me, I will put up at the Trevor Arms, and renew our intimacy so pleasantly made in town.

           " Yours most sincerely,

                 " C. NORTON."

" I know Miss Priscilla is very anxious to let 'The Willows,'" said Victor, as he returned the letter to Warre. " I should say you had better go up and see her about it at once. I am so glad to see you back, George. I wish you were not so much away."

Then Victor went off to the timber-yard, and George Warre to the Manor House.

Miss Priscilla liked young Warre because Victor liked him. She regretted that Victor should not have a better stamp of friend than the landlord's son ; but he was at least an honest, manly fellow, even if he was rather rough and noisy. She received him, there-fore, graciously, and having read Mr. Norton's letter, said she knew of no objection to receiving Mrs. Astor as her tenant, and that he might telegraph to Mr. Norton to that effect.

In high feather at his success, George Warre went off to the telegraph-office, and at one o'clock that day Con Norton informed Mrs. Astor and her sister that " The Willows " would be ready for them on the 1st of July.

Young Warre was of a talkative disposition, and was very proud of the friendship of this young London swell he had picked up at Bill Nash's. The result was that all Olton Priors was on the tip-toe of expectation and excitement about the new-comers before they arrived in the place at all.

Rumour of course exaggerated everything that Norton had said or implied in his letter. Warre told Broughton, and Broughton told his wife and Miss Spink, who gossiped to

the Hunts and the Howards, who retailed
the news, with enlargements of their own, to
every one whom they happened to meet.

By the time Norton and the two ladies
arrived, it was all over the town that a
widow of enormous wealth, and her sister
—who was the belle of the London season—
had taken "The Willows" for a year, and
curiosity to see them ran high throughout
Olton Priors.

Norton, in the meantime, had employed
himself in getting together material for what
he was pleased to call his "Provincial Tour."
He was an accomplished man in many ways,
a fair musician and a painter in water-colours.
He took care to have in his portmanteau a
choice assortment of all the newest songs, to
please all tastes, and as sketching in Sandshire would give him an excuse for prolong-
ing his stay, if he found it agreeable, he
provided himself with painting materials also.

Before the trio left London there was some discussion about the adoption of names. Astor had already been assumed by the lady who bore that surname, and Norton was the "alias" that Conrad had chosen for this particular year of grace; but Liz Mullins had been Liz Mullins these many years. As Eliza Mullins she had pocketed the five hundred, the thousand, and the three hundred pounds as compensation for her blighted affections; as Eliza Mullins she had hooked the brother of the idiot girl at Folkestone, and Jenkyns and Hopkins in London, therefore it was desirable that before opening a fresh campaign, Eliza Mullins should choose another designation.

"As our provincial tour is chiefly undertaken on Mr. Broom's account," said Norton, "I think Liz should consider his probable tastes in her assumption of a name. Descent from some branch of the *haute noblesse* might help to arrange matters. Suppose we change 'Eliza' into 'Élise,' and 'Mullins' into 'Desmoulines.' How would that do?"

The alteration fell in with Liz Mullins's views, and so that matter was speedily settled.

" The Willows" was a pretty cottage standing back from the high-road between Olton Priors and the Priory, at the foot of the hill on which the parish church was built. Several large weeping-willows in the small garden between the cottage and the road shut out the street beyond, and had probably given the cottage its present name. At the back of the house was a good garden, a coach-house and stable, and a poultry-yard, and beyond these again a small orchard. At the other side of the orchard was a lane called Love Lane, the banks of which were celebrated for violets and primroses in spring, and was a favourite walk with the good

people of **Olton Priors all** the year round.
This lane eventually **led** into Shalebourne
Wood, and through that to the right bank
of the Shale, where it joined the main road
between Olton Priors and Shalemouth.

The Manor House **was but a stone's** throw
from " The Willows," and had probably at
one **time** formed part of the same property.
It stood **on the** same side **of** the street, **a**
little nearer **to** the **Priory, a** little **farther**
from the **town.**

Miss Priscilla **of course knew nothing**
more of her new tenants than what she had
heard from George Warre, but she wished to
show them some civility on their arrival, so
Beer was sent **to " The Willows "** with a
basket of fruit and vegetables, **and** an enor-
mous bouquet **of roses,** with Miss Priscilla
Trevor's compliments.

Miss Priscilla had herself been over to
" The Willows " in **the** afternoon of that

day to see that everything was comfortable
for the " *soi-disant* widow " and her lovely
sister.   Two respectable women had been
engaged as cook and housemaid respectively,
" The Willows " had been swept and gar-
nished, and the 1st of July saw Mrs. Astor
and her sister, Miss Desmoulines, well settled
in at the cottage.

CHAPTER V.

O N the Sunday following the arrival of the new-comers, the parish church was fuller than usual. It had leaked out through the servants at the "The Willows," that Mrs. Astor and Miss Desmoulines would attend morning service there, and not at St. Mark's ; so even the Howards, who usually attended the latter place of worship, because it was nearer Arundel Lodge, trudged up the hill to the parish church on this particular Sunday morning.

Miss Priscilla waited to give her tenants "time to turn themselves," as she expressed it to Barker, before calling upon them; but she sent a message to "The Willows" on Saturday night, to say that if the ladies liked to avail themselves of seats in her pew, there would be two at their disposal on the following day. The offer was accepted. Mrs. Astor found out from her servants that Miss Priscilla's pew was in the chancel, close up by the altar-rails, and that she would therefore have to walk the whole length of the church to it from the usual entrance.

This was satisfactory. Mrs. Astor timed her movements so as to arrive at church in the middle of the Psalms, when every one was standing up, and the high old-fashioned pews were not in the way of those who might wish to see her.

She was dressed in widow's mourning, with a widow's cap beneath her bonnet which became her *mignonne* face extremely well ; and Miss Desmoulines, as we must now call her, followed her sister up the aisle in a magpie costume of black and white silk and a marabout feather in her bonnet.

All eyes were turned on them as they sailed up the aisle to Miss Priscilla's pew. Mrs. Astor's veil was down, and she walked with an air of pensive mournfulness ; but Élise looked strikingly handsome, and fully bore out the reports of her beauty which had reached Olton Priors through the medium of George Warre.

Mr. Norton had not accompanied the ladies. He had deemed it inexpedient to be seen with them at first. He did not wish it to be supposed possible that he was in Olton Priors as a lover. That might interfere with the ladies' designs in other quarters ; and, besides, he had his own fish to fry elsewhere.

As the ladies took their places, Miss Pris-

cilla made them a formal little bow, inti-
mating that she was the proprietor of the
pew.   Mrs. Astor inclined herself mourn-
fully, Élise bowed smilingly, and all the con-
gregation took it for granted that Miss
Priscilla had "taken up" the new arrivals;
otherwise they would not have been seated
in her pew.

After service was over Miss Priscilla introduced herself; hoped they had found
"The Willows" to their taste, and expressed
her willingness to call if Mrs. Astor yet felt
equal to receiving visitors.   The sisters on
their part were in modulated raptures with
"The Willows," the neighbourhood, the
scenery, and everything connected with
Olton Priors that had yet come under their
notice.   They thanked Miss Priscilla with
much *empressement*, and said they should be
delighted to see her whenever she could find
time to pay them a visit.

"As far as I am concerned," said Mrs. Astor with a sigh, "I am more than content to enjoy the retirement of this country life ; but I fear my sister may find it dull, so I must bestir myself for her sake. We must not be selfish even in our grief, must we ?" and Mrs. Astor had suffered the ghost of a pensive smile to play upon her lips for a moment ; but it was quickly repressed, and the veil was lowered to prevent the outer world from being saddened by the sight of her fictitious grief.

"Poor young woman," said Miss Priscilla to Barker on her return from church ; "we must think of something to cheer her, Barker. So young, too, to be a widow, and with such a sweet childish face !"

"Remarkable old cat !" said Élise to Anne as they entered the gate of "The Willows." "She has taken quite a fancy to you, my dear ; if we work this country under her auspices, I predict we shall be a huge success."

Conrad Norton came to luncheon, and stayed at "The Willows" for the remainder of the day. The Broughtons and Miss Spink had met him in the street as he came up from the "Trevor Arms;" so had the Howard girls as they returned to Arundel Lodge from the parish church. The ladies were in raptures with his appearance. So distinguished! so thorough-bred! so remarkably handsome! so perfectly dressed! Such was the opinion of one and all. That George Warre should be on intimate terms with such a man, sent up the landlord's son several rungs in the social ladder at Olton Priors.

"Have you run down any game?" said Élise as the trio took their seats in the dining-room. "These first few days have been marvellously dull, I must confess."

" I have employed myself in reconnoitering merely," answered Conrad; " but I am well pleased. The country is alive with game of all sorts, and if we play our cards properly we ought to make a large bag."

" Have you picked up another Augustus Darell ?" asked Mrs. Astor.

" Certainly not, and don't want to ; I am a Mentor of morals here, never touch cards, and am averse to all games of chance, never indulge in 'nips,' and have abjured B. and S. as injurious to the system."

" Take care you don't overdo your part," said Élise, laughing. " Remember you are a man about town, and a frequenter of Bill Nash's, the Roehampton pet."

" Trust me ; I was not born yesterday. There is a bottle of brandy in my bedroom and a syphon of seltzer on my table. It is being constantly seen in the bar that damns a man."

"Have you seen Lady Margate yet?" inquired Mrs. Astor.

"No; Lord Margate and his brother are going to be away to-morrow on the trial trip of their new steam-launch. I have ascertained that Lady Margate usually walks in the Coddesley woods for an hour before luncheon daily, and I shall take my chance of meeting her there. If I fail in that, I shall go to the house and ask for her."

"You did not tell us anything of Lord Margate's brother," said Élise. "Is he married, or is there a chance in his direction for Anne or me?"

"None for you, certainly; and I do not think he is the sort of man who would readily fall into a trap. I have never seen him, but I hear he is a keen, smart man of the world, who has spent some ten years in a crack cavalry regiment, and is not easily taken in. No! I do not think it would be worth while for either of you to waste time over Captain Norman."

"This young Broom-sprig won't do for two of us," said Élise. "Unless there are other men in the market, it will be dull work for the one whom Mr. Plantagenet does not condescend to fancy. Who else are available, even for amusement?"

"Well! there's the ritualistic curate, and the young 'sawbones' who has just started in business here as a surgeon; and there is Victor Ross, a timber-merchant, whom I have been introduced to by Warre, and who is a sort of young Viking, or Norse demigod, with a yellow beard and the proportions of a son of Anak. Then there is Warre himself, a well set-up young ruffian, but more at home at Bill Nash's than in a drawing-room. I have heard of others too, but only vaguely. There are some sons of a Colonel Lane of Pegwell, and some young Careys of Shalebourne Manor; but the Broom-sprig is *the* 'tip,' and all the running must be made in that direction. If one of you could manage a real 'Platonic' with Norman, it would do more good than harm; but I may as well say at once, that my object is to keep that young man unmarried!"

"Keep him unmarried!" exclaimed both the sisters in a breath. "And pray, why?"

Conrad Norton bit his lip. "That is my affair," he said, in a very disagreeable tone. "You have your little games; I have mine. If you expect me to help you in yours, you must do your best for me in return. I hope Norman will never marry, and I shall put a spoke in his wheel whenever he tries. However, I cannot explain my reasons at present, and, if you have no objection, I think I will light a cigar. Come and show me over your new demesne."

CHAPTER VI.

ON the following day, Lady Margate, ignorant of her danger, took a book into the woods as usual, about noon, when she had seen her husband and his brother off for their excursion to Shalemouth in the new steam-launch.

It was a bright, hot day; but there was a breeze from the south-east coming up from the sea, and Lady Margate, choosing a spot which commanded the river, was soon immersed in the pages of her novel.

The woods round Coddesley were not large, and Conrad had not much difficulty in discovering that part of them which a lady would be likely to choose for a morning ramble.

He had dressed with scrupulous care. His clothes fitted him to perfection. He had never looked handsomer or better got-up than when he strolled out of Olton Priors, in the direction of Coddesley woods.

As he reached a turn in the road that skirted the woods, he saw Lady Margate, book in hand, sitting on a rustic bench beneath a giant oak. His opportunity was come. Almost before she was aware of any one's presence, he stepped out from the surrounding trees, and said, in a clear, cheerful voice :

" How do you do, Maggie ?"

She started up with a slight scream. The book she had been reading dropped from her

hands.   A deadly pallor stole over her face
as she drew herself up with as much dignity
as she could command; but her trembling
lips refused to articulate a sound.

He advanced nearer to her, and held out
his hand.

" Your greeting is not very cordial," said
he jauntily.   " I am afraid I have taken
you by surprise.   Being in the neighbourhood for a few weeks, I thought I would pay
you a visit.   Come, Maggie, haven't you a
pleasant word to say to a fellow after all
these years ?"

He came closer still.   Then she found
voice at last:

" Do not touch me," she gasped, half
choked with terror and emotion.   " Conway
Norbury, you are a scoundrel and a villain."

" Gently ! my dear child, gently.   You
should never suffer yourself to call a gentleman names."

"A gentleman! You a gentleman!" she cried, with scathing scorn. "You! a seducer, a liar, a——"

"Quite so, quite so," said he, with the same careless air of assumed indifference; "all that is quite true; but you seem to have quite forgotten who believed the lies, and who was the person who suffered."

She cowered away from him in horror and loathing, hiding her face in her hands.

"Why have you come here?" she cried wildly. "What have I done that I should be cursed with your blighting presence? I am a married woman now; the wife of a man who can, and will, protect me. Why should I fear you?"

"Why, indeed?" said he. "You are exciting yourself quite unnecessarily, I assure you, Maggie. You have nothing to fear from me; absolutely nothing."

"You lie!" she said fiercely. "Did you

not want, you would not have cared to track me. Is it not enough that you blasted my youth? Must you canker my whole life with your hate?"

"It was not hate then, Maggie; and it is not hate now. I want nothing that you cannot easily grant. I do not ask for money; I have plenty for my needs. I do not seek to expose what, for my own sake, had best be kept secret. If you will only listen calmly, you will see that I want but a little thing."

"Then you do want. I knew you must, or you would not have acted the sleuth-hound as you have."

"I do want something. I want your silence. That is not much to ask. Silence for silence. No word of mine shall ever be let fall which can affect your good name, if you will consent to receive me as simply an old friend. Circumstances have made it ab-

solutely necessary that I should stay in this
neighbourhood for a few weeks, perhaps
longer. I find it dull. I know no one, or
next to no one. I must have society
and amusement. You have but to recog-
nise in me an old acquaintance, and I
will build up for you such a reputation as
might get you canonised. If you will
not——"

"Well, what then?" said she, with a fine
sneer.

"Then I will upset your house of cards
with a mere fillip of my finger, with one
breath of my lips."

"You cannot! I defy you! You have
been a liar from the first; you are a liar now.
Conway Norbury is not your name, and
never was your name. Under that name
you persuaded me to leave home and family
and friends. Then you deserted me, and
left me for another woman. Had it not

been for Lord Margate I should have perished in my utter destitution."

"I think you have sense enough to see," said he, "that it would not be pleasant for you, or the noble earl, your husband, to have such a scandal at your very doors as I could bring about your ears if I so pleased. You seem to forget all the letters I have in my possession from you. Keep your title; keep your husband; keep this remarkably pretty place in which you are living in such ease and luxury. All I want is your countenance in Sandshire. I do not think this is much to ask.'

Then he lifted his dark, lustrous eyes to hers, and fixed them on her. Though his words were honey-sweet, his eyes were pitilessly cruel.

"What is it you want me to do?" she asked, in a hoarse voice.

"Some friends of mine, who are in deep

distress, have come down here to recover their
spirits.   One is a widow, a Mrs. Astor; she
is accompanied by her sister, a Miss Desmoulines.   They are ladies, and agreeable women.
I wish you to make yourself pleasant to them,
call on them, ask them here, and generally be-
friend them."

" How am I to know what sort of people
they may be ?" asked Lady Margate.

" How are they *not* to know what sort of
person you may be ?" he retorted sneeringly.

" For how long do these people require my
countenance ?"

" They have taken 'The Willows' for
three months; they might, of course, stay
longer; but it is so very unlikely, that I may
say I am certain their stay will end then."

" What are these people to you ?" she asked.

" That is my own secret," he replied.

" Look here," she said, suddenly confronting
him with more courage than she had hitherto

been able to summon. " Lord Margate knows that there had been an unhappy side to my history, for I told him before I married him."

" The more fool you," said he.

" I think not," she continued. " Anything you could say would not change my position in his eyes, would not imperil my rank, or sever me from my husband's love. If you choose to spread the story of your own infamy and my shame in Sandshire, we should have to leave the county, which I abominate, and perhaps the country, for which I have no particular liking. That is the worst you can do."

" That is the worst I can do," he repeated coolly.

Her eyes flashed with suppressed rage. Whatever there was of evil in this woman was being rapidly drawn to the surface by the man's calm insolence.

" You have my letters ?" she continued.

" About twenty of them," he replied.

" I have a fancy to have them back, and I know I must pay my price. Name it, and give them back."

" I am not in want of money," he said, with contemptuous indifference; " I told you so before. My terms are these: silence for silence. By silence I do not mean a mere withholding of our real knowledge of each other; I mean a cordial support of each other's pretentions to being respectable people. On your part, you must not only deny all knowledge of anything against me, but allow me to play my own game in this neighbourhood without let or hindrance. On my part, I will pledge myself to lie on your behalf as—well—as successfully as I can lie! and I will give you back your letters this day three months, and clear out of the place for good and all."

" And these friends of yours, these adventuresses, am I to countenance them too?"

" Certainly, they will do you no harm.

They are women of tolerably good birth and education; they are living in a house belonging to a Miss Priscilla Trevor, in Olton Priors, who has already taken them by the hand. All you need do is to follow the old lady's lead."

" And my purgatory shall only last three months—that you will swear ?"

" If by 'your purgatory' you mean my presence in Sandshire, it will only last three months; that I will swear."

" I have no pledge that you will keep your promise."

" Look you, Maggie, I am perfectly aware that I should not dream of telling you the truth, if I had any purpose to serve in telling you a lie. That I have a purpose to effect in this neighbourhood is obvious. You know me well enough to be aware I should not kick my heels in this deadly-lively hole for nothing. But that purpose has nothing, absolutely no-

thing to do with you. I do not want your
money. I am perfectly aware Lord Margate
is not rich. Such sums as I could wring from
him, just to hold my tongue about our little
—flirtation, shall we call it?—in the past,
would not satisfy me, even if he chose to
' part' rather than leave Coddesley. Besides,
it would not suit me to live on such means.
I have turned over a new leaf."

" Not a better one I'll be bound," said she.

" Perhaps not, but at any rate a new one,
in which only the highest code of morality is
to be found. To live on the pickings of your
husband's scanty fortune would not suit me ;
so just make your mind easy on that score.
For once I am telling you the real honest
truth. Promise me not only that you will not
put a spoke in my wheel, but that you will
back me up when I want your countenance
and support, and I will promise that, at
the end of three months, you shall have

your letters back, and be quit of me for ever."

"I must know your purpose before I consent," she said, though in truth she knew that she would have to give way to the terms of this adventurous scoundrel.

"As yet it is not definite enough for me to put it into words. I was anxious to keep out of the way for a time, and yet not die of dulness. London is too hot for me at present, and Paris is hotter still. I found that my friends, Mrs. Astor and her sister, thought of coming here for the summer months, and I elected to come too. Then I find my little Maggie established in the neighbourhood as a leader of society and the wife of an earl. I must either pack up my traps and go, or effect a compromise with my old friend. As I did not wish to go, I came up here to see you and offer my terms. Take them or refuse them, as you please; but if you refuse them,

I will make Sandshire too hot to hold you in less than a week."

She leaned her white face upon her trembling hands and tried to think. He stood against the oak, his legs crossed, his hands in his pockets, looking coolly defiant and imperturbable. She knew she must give way. She had thought at first he wanted money. Had it been so, she would have told Lord Margate the truth at once and left the matter in his hands; but the villain had either foreseen this or was in no need of funds. "Silence for silence," those were his terms; but then she must deceive her husband; at any rate she must keep him in the dark. Could she bring herself to do this? On the other hand, could she bear the disgrace of discovery? A countess occupies a social pedestal. She knew that this man would carry out his threat, if she baulked him, and then even her shreds of fair fame would be torn from her, and her shame would be notorious throughout all that country-side.

"You did not show such squeamishness when we first met at Cremorne," said he, by way of jogging her recollection of all that he could tell if he were so minded. "I should have thought a woman who has lived the life you have, with all its 'ups' and 'downs,' would have understood what 'silence for silence' meant."

"I do understand," she gasped, "but I have been happy, oh! so happy! since those horrible days, that I cannot get quickly back into the hell in which you still choose to live, and into which you would drag me, if you could. I accept your terms, so long as you keep within the bounds of your own bargain, but if you touch me or mine with your poisonous breath, I will throw my own good name to the winds in the mere hope of

crushing you; and there are things in your
past life that they might like to hear at
Scotland Yard, things which I could tell
them."

"Pray spare your threats," said he with
an evil smile. "They do not affect the
question or me; do I understand you to
say that you accept my terms?"

"Yes! so long as you keep your word."

"Then I may expect that you will find
out for yourself that I am staying at the
Trevor Arms, and that I am a distant cousin
whom you have not seen for years? also that
you will call on Mrs. Astor and ask us all to
this house, and in due course present us to
society as your own friends?"

"Yes," she cried, "you may."

"My name is Conrad Norton at present,"
he said, "very much at your ladyship's
service."

Then with an insolent laugh he offered her

his card. " In case you might not recollect
the change of name," he said. " Now I will
relieve you of my presence ; I presume I
may intimate to my friends that you will call
on them this week ?"

" Yes !" she answered faintly, as she
dropped on to the seat where he had first
found her. " I will call and I will write to
you ; now, I beseech you, go !"

He made her a mocking bow, turned on
his heel, and disappeared among the trees.

With a little groan of smothered agony,
she threw herself on the ground and sobbed
as though her heart would break.

CHAPTER VII.

HOW MAGGIE LAWRENCE BECAME A COUNTESS.

THERE had been a time when Lady Margate had not known what "nerves" meant. She was, as she admitted, a farmer's daughter, and the rude healthfulness of her girlish days knew nothing of hysteria and such kinds of nervous ailments.

As Margaret Lawrence she had been a gay, happy, strong girl, inclined to value finery and pleasure at too high a rate, but with nothing really bad in her character.

When she was about nineteen, her parents had allowed her to visit some relations living at Battersea, people who kept a confectioner's shop, and who drove a thriving trade. The daughters of the confectioner served in the shop, and it was mainly due to their fascinations of manner and appearance that the place had acquired such notoriety in the neighbourhood.

Though the girls were coquettish, they were perfectly well able to take care of themselves. They were London-bred and accustomed to take gentlemen's compliments for what they were worth; but their pretty cousin, Maggie Lawrence, who helped them during her visit to Battersea, knew nothing of London men and their ways, and she very easily lost her heart to a dashing young fellow who frequently looked in at the confectioner's, and who was known to the girls as Mr. Conway Norbury.

Mr. Norbury was perfectly heartless and unscrupulous. The girl's evident admiration fanned a passing fancy into a flame. In company with her cousins, Maggie Lawrence had occasionally gone to Cremorne; there Norbury had a wider field for action than in the confectioner's shop. She was very young, very credulous, and madly in love with the smart Adonis who vowed an undying affection for her. The story is too sadly common to need dwelling upon. Under promise of marriage he had ruined her, lived with her till his fancy had tired, and when she had wearied him by importunity for a marriage ceremony, left her to live or die as might be. He had gone abroad, far out of her reach; and she had been left, with but little money and no knowledge of the hardness of the world to girls in her position, to struggle on as best she could.

The temptation to fall lower than she had

already fallen necessarily became stronger and stronger as the few bits of jewellery and finery she had went one by one to the pawn-shop; but Maggie Lawrence, though she had listened to the vows of a man whom she had passionately loved, would not, and did not, succumb to the life of infamy that lay open to her. She had struggled on for some time in rags and almost starving, but at last one of the gay young fellows whom she had remembered at the shop in Battersea happened to meet her in the street, and paused in surprise at seeing her in such a plight. To him she had told her tale. The young man was capable of dis-criminating between misfortune and vice. Moreover, he happened to be a gentle-man. He helped her liberally in a manner that could carry no offence. He procured work for her, or pretended to do so when the work could not be really found. On one occasion he had offered to take her to the theatre, and Maggie, whose life was one of dull routine, had allowed herself to go. Her friend was accompanied by Lord Margate, to whom the young man had told the girl's unhappy history. The impression she had made on the young nobleman that night was so strong that in a month from that date he offered to marry her, and the poor half-starved victim of Norbury's cruel treachery became the wife of a peer of the realm.

The mutual friend, who had been present at the wedding, was no other than Dolly Darell.

The poverty and trials of that time, before Dolly Darell had relieved her necessities, had, however, greatly altered Maggie Law-rence's constitution for the worse, and when, as Lady Margate, a life of ease and luxury had been her lot, the suddenness of the un-expected change had again had a bad effect upon her nervous system. For she was called upon, daily and hourly, to play a part, to acquit herself before society as was proper for Lord Margate's wife ; and the strain of the attempt, which had by no means always been attended with success, had, over and over again, been too much for her.

But now that there was real danger to herself, to the husband whom she had learnt to love with honest fondness, and to his family, Lady Margate felt some of the hardness of her most bitter days come back to her. When the first paroxysm of grief and terror had spent itself, she found herself better able to cope with the misery of her present situation than she had imagined possible before the man she had so dreaded had actually tracked her.

Most woes are worse in prospect than in reality. The nervous terrors that had hitherto haunted and tormented Lady Margate were over now. Nothing worse, she thought, could happen to her than what had happened already; and with this belief came courage and nerve, and daring even, such as she had not experienced since the days when she rose at five o'clock and milked the cows at her father's humble farm.

She hesitated for some time whether it would not be really best to tell her husband that this snake in the grass had crept into her path again; but she knew the character of Conrad Norton too well for her to follow up this line of action. He might be forced to quit Olton Priors certainly; but she was sure that he would only do so after emptying his poison fangs upon her character. If he did this, she and her husband would have to leave Coddesley and Sandshire; and Lord Margate cared only now, in his failing health, to live upon his own estate.

She would have been happier far away

from Olton Priors and the people who had received her with so great suspicion and distrust; but she knew that Lord Margate hoped to end his days within the gates of his ancestral home.

On the following day, therefore, she casually mentioned that a connection of hers was staying at the Trevor Arms, whom she wished to take some notice of; and she said that as Mrs. Astor and Miss Desmoulines were friends of his, she thought she would call upon them.

Lord Margate never questioned his wife about her movements or her reasons for action; besides, he was of so easy-going and unsuspicious a nature, that he took very little notice of the remark, except to say, as he usually did: "Oh! really—well, you had better ask them to dinner."

Lady Margate left a note at the Trevor Arms, on her way to "The Willows." It

was not often that she used the barouche and
pair; she much preferred driving herself in
her pony-carriage; but she rightly guessed
that it was unlikely Conrad would have let
these women into his secret, and that though
they might make shrewd guesses of an un-
pleasant nature, she would do most wisely in
keeping up at first some distance and reserve.

To this end she drove up to the gate of
"The Willows" with considerable ostenta-
tion; so much so, that all the street knew
that the Countess of Margate had called on
the new arrivals. The ladies, however, were
out. Relieved by this reprieve, she went on
to see Miss Priscilla, who had found Mrs.
Astor and her sister at home the day before,
and who was consequently able to give Lady
Margate some account of their manners and
appearance.

Miss Priscilla, it appeared, had been much

taken with the widow, who had seemed to be, quite unable to rouse herself from her deep grief; but the old lady's comments on Miss Desmoulines were far from flattering, though she admitted that the girl was very hand- some and had made herself sufficiently agree- able.

" I hope I have not done wrong, Lady Margate, in accepting tenants of whom I know nothing," said Miss Priscilla. " I have a respect for George Warre, because Victor likes him; and as he seemed to be certain that Mr. Norton and his friends were nice people, I did not like to be too particular."

Lady Margate wondered if Mrs. Astor was of the same sort as Conrad; and if so, she inwardly pitied Miss Priscilla.

CHAPTER VIII.

THE SHALEFORD CLUB.

FOR some years past an archery club had existed in Olton Priors. There had been also a cricket club, and, for social purposes, these two had been lately amalgamated.

The club was managed by a secretary, a treasurer, and a lady paramount, who held office for one year only, and were not eligible for re-election until the third year after their previous tenure of office.

The ground originally occupied by this

club had been a level field at the foot of what was then known as Mambury Common; but the common had lately been cut up into sections, of which Buncombe was one, and at the present time everything north of Buncombe had practically ceased to be part of the common, and had become the property of various owners.

The field in which the archery and cricket clubs had been wont to assemble had been bought by Mr. Broom, who offered it free of rent to the club during the summer and autumn months, and thereby gained some popularity on his first arrival in Sandshire.

The club was now called the Shaleford Club. Archery meetings and cricket matches were held on its grounds on alternate Wednesdays; and once in every month the amusements terminated in a dance, in a pavilion built for the purpose.

The club was originally an Olton Priors affair, and consequently most of the people who belonged to the place had been members from the first; but as it increased in popularity, it was found necessary to limit the number of members, and to establish the ballot. Directly membership became difficult, every-one in that part of Sandshire felt the necessity of establishing their claims to position by demanding admittance to the Shaleford Club. It speedily became the fashion. A list of rules and regulations was printed and distributed; would-be leaders of society offered handsome prizes; enterprising trades-men followed suit; crack elevens began to send challenges to the Shaleford Club; a special cricket-ground was laid down, with chalk beneath the turf; the club started a many-coloured ribbon, and the fame of the Shaleford monthly gatherings began to spread far and wide.

Popularity begot exclusiveness, exclusiveness heart-burnings and hostility. A social line of demarcation sprang into existence between those who were, and those who were not, members of the Shaleford Club, and party spirit ran very high. The original members were sometimes people who did not occupy such social position as entitled them to rank among the county families, but they could not be turned out, and they were perpetually at loggerheads with the exclusive party about the admission of fresh members. The " counter," in short, black-balled the " county," and the " county" the " counter." Naturally enough, no one admitted that his family belonged to the " counter " set; but when that family held no acre of ground, occupied no county position, and were altogether very little people living in a very small way, to set up for being " county " people became obviously absurd.

This third class preserved the balance between "county" and "counter" in the Shaleford Club. Sometimes it sided with "county," sometimes with "counter," and on the whole was equally disliked by both.

People who have made their fortunes, and have come to settle in a new district, have always the chance of improving upon their past social position, if their education warrants their advancement.

This had been the case with the Brooms, who, by virtue of a combination of money, wits, and impudence, had penetrated far into the central circles of Sandshire society. Still they had not reached the highest rungs of the ladder yet, and the ambition of the "House of Anjou" was far from being satisfied.

In the present year, however, Mr. Broom was Secretary, Lady Margate Lady Paramount, and Mr. Broughton Treasurer to the Shaleford Club. A new pavilion, capable of holding three hundred people, had been presented to the club by Mr. Broom, for dancing purposes, and, in consequence, it had been suggested that more members should be invited to join the Club.

The Brooms being *nouveaux riches,* had done all they could to prevent the enrolment into the club of people of their own station. Many a name that Lady Margate had allowed to stand was scratched off the list by Mr. Broom, under his wife's direction. Lady Margate herself was but a puppet, Mrs. Broom pulled the strings. Mrs. Broom had not called on Mrs. Broughton, or rather she had behaved in such a manner to the latter, that Mrs. Broughton had felt it was impossible to be on visiting terms with Mrs. Broom. Broughton himself—being a keen man of business, with an eye to having the management of the Buncombe estates some day or other—toadied the Brooms on every possible occasion ; but his wife never forgot or forgave Mrs. Broom's rudeness, and, backed up by her sister, Miss Spink, kept up a petty warfare against the Broom party.

As Mr. Broughton, the Treasurer of the Shaleford Club, always gave way to Mr. Broom, the Secretary, the two men got on well enough in their collaboration ; but when a new set of members were to be balloted for, the wives interfered, and Olton Priors society was shaken to its centre.

The wrangling had reached such a pitch, that the club had suggested to Lady Margate, as Lady Paramount, the necessity of calling a committee of ladies together, who should decide, in a friendly way, if possible, the titles of their candidates to election as members.

To this course Lady Margate had been only too glad to accede. A day in the first week of July had been fixed for the committee to assemble at the Trevor Arms, and there the tug of war was to be settled, if possible, once for all.

Mr. Broom, as Secretary, took the chair. The Lady Paramount sat on his right hand, Mrs. Broom on his left. At the other end of the table Mr. Broughton sat, as Treasurer, flanked by his wife and Mrs. Lane of Pegwell. There was a great mixture, for the original members of the club had mustered in great force, and many of them belonged to a set who had no footing in Sandshire society at all.

Among these was Mrs. Hunt, the spirited wife of the paper manufacturer at Shaleford Mills. The Hunts were at daggers drawn with Lord and Lady Margate, who objected to the erection of tall chimneys fifty yards from their park palings, and they were hardly more friendly towards the Brooms, who had emphatically declined to place them on their visiting list.

Mrs. Hunt was backed up by all the old "counter" set of Olton Priors, who resented Mrs. Broom's airs, and by the professional men's wives, such as Mrs. Broughton, Mrs. Bremridge—the wife of Mr. Broughton's partner—and others.

Lady Margate, as Lady Paramount, had no vote at all; she had nothing to do but to issue the notices, distribute the prizes, and keep the peace, the last of which she found an uncommonly hard task.

Mr. Broom made an introductory speech at some length, in which he pointed out the inadvisability of having recourse to the ballot, if the committee could settle among themselves who would be the persons most

agreeable to them as new members of the
Shaleford Club.

He then read out a list of names that had
been submitted to the Lady Paramount for
selection. He said that each name on his
list had been duly proposed and seconded by
members of the club; but as it was an un-
pleasant duty to have to inform an intending
candidate that his room was preferred to his
company, this committee had been formed to
learn the feelings of the club with regard to
the persons proposed.

The list was a long one, and contained the
names of Mr. Trevor, of the Priory; Mr.
Victor Ross, of Black Rock; Captain Charles
Norman, of Coddesley; Mr. Howard, of
Arundel Lodge; the Rev. Celestine Chan-
ning, curate of St. Marks; Mr. Pericles
Bone; Mr. Hedgering, of Shalemouth; Sir
Rufus MacGregor, of Shalemouth; Mr.
Boodle, of Shalemouth; Mr. Herries, of

Applecombe Farm ; Mr. Pryce Tynker, of Pegwell Barn ; and Mr. Moggs, the manager of the Potteries at Bossy-Compton.

"The gentlemen whose names he had read out," Mr. Broom said, "were of course understood to stand for their families. Any elected member had the right to bring not only his own immediate family to the Archery and Cricket Club, but any guests who might be staying beneath his own roof; also every member had the right to invite, as guests, any two persons, other than those already mentioned, to the monthly dance in the pavilion.

Then Mr. Broom sat down and mopped his heated face, and a perfect buzz of comment on, and objection to, the candidates filled the room from end to end. The ladies rose from the table and collected in groups in the corners of the room, sometimes changing over to hear the opinions of some rival faction, sometimes asking for information from the Secretary or the Lady Paramount. At last matters seemed to have settled themselves; Mrs. Broom and Mrs. Broughton made separate communications to Lady Margate, a few other ladies did the same, and Mr. Broom, instructed by the Lady Paramount, rose to his legs to express the general feeling of the committee on the subject.

Mr. Broom said that he had been deputed to " bell the cat " so to speak, and he hoped it was understood that he was merely the spokesman for the committee generally. He begged to announce that the desire to accept as new members the following gentlemen was almost unanimous; and he then mentioned Messrs. Trevor, Channing, Herries and Tynker, and Captain Norman. He further stated that Messrs. Hedgering and Boodle, with Sir Rufus MacGregor, had been almost as unanimously rejected, and that he was sorry to say that party feeling ran so high about the election, or non-election of the remaining candidates, that the matter would have to be referred to the ballot. As far as he could gather, the proposers and seconders of the gentlemen, whose names for membership were under discussion, had declined to withdraw their nominees, which, in his opinion, would have been the wisest course to pursue; but since they had come to a determination to decide the matter by ballot, he had nothing more to say than that he hoped every member of the club would kindly be present that day week, in the same room, for that purpose. He hoped that it was generally known that every member of a family belonging to the club, who was over twenty-one, had a right to vote; but not the guests who might happen to be with them at the time.

Then Mr. Broom declared the meeting

adjourned for a week, and "county" and "counter" descended the staircase of the Trevor Arms in a condition of smothered animosity, which was destined to produce very bitter feuds before the week was out.

Of course it soon leaked out in a small country town like Olton Priors, what the objections to each family were, and who had made them. This caused a great deal of ill-feeling in the neighbourhood. Mr. Hedgering of Shalemouth was so notoriously quarrelsome that "county" and "counter" alike preferred his room to his company; and Sir Rufus MacGregor had for years gone by the nickname of the "Bear with a sore head" throughout Sandshire. Mr. Boodle was not in a social position to belong to an archery club at all, and everybody was extremely incensed against the Hunts for proposing him, and the Broughtons for seconding his nomination. There was the same feeling with regard to Mr. Moggs, though it had not been sufficiently strongly expressed to induce Mr. Broom to strike his name off the list at once.   Mrs. Broom herself had been heard to say that if the Pottery manager was admitted to the club, she should leave it; and there were others who expressed their opinion in much the same terms.

Mr. Pericles Bone was an offensive young snob; the ladies of Olton Priors did not quite go so far as to call him so, in so many words, but he was extremely unpopular with men, both old and young.   He again had been a nominee of Messrs. Hunt and Broughton, who represented a combination of trades-people and professional men, as distinct from the landed proprietors, the clergy, and officers of the army and navy.

Mr. Howard again was a " counter " candidate ; but on the other hand he had not made his money in the place, and he was, in a small way, a landed proprietor himself. The exclusion of Mr. Howard would mean the exclusion of his daughters, and although Mrs. Broom would have been glad if the Howards had been excluded from the first, yet Mr. Broom and Genista would be sure to vote upon the Howard side.

Victor Ross had been nominated very much against his inclination as a candidate for membership. He was fond of cricket, and an uncommonly good bat, but he thought archery a very poor sort of amusement, and he did not care for dancing. Captain Norman had over-persuaded him, however, at Miss Priscilla's garden-party, and Lord Margate himself had proposed him.

Up to the present time Lord and Lady Margate had hardly known of the existence of the Ross family, and it was with considerable surprise that Lord Margate learnt from his brother that Victor and he had been at Rugby together. Since Miss Priscilla's garden-party, however, Captain Norman had been continually singing the praises of the young timber-merchant, and regretting that such a splendid-looking fellow should not enter more into the society for which his education had fitted him. One result had been that Lord Margate had proposed Victor for the Shaleford Club, and another that Captain Norman had asked him, in Lord Margate's name, to dine at Coddesley to meet the Trevors.

When the "counter," however, became aware that Victor Ross was a "county" nominee, the hitherto passive dislike to the young man began to take an active form. It was remembered against him that his father had once been a carpenter, before he first went to Canada; that his grandfather had been a mechanic all his life, and that his grandmother was only the daughter of a small farmer. That Tom Ross should have married above him, was an additional ground for dislike among such people as the Hunts and the Broughtons. The Ross family were suddenly discovered to have given themselves airs. They had for years declined to mix with "their betters," as the Hunt and Broughton faction undoubtedly considered themselves; and that they should now be "cheek by jowl" with such people as Lord Margate and Lady Adela Trevor, was not to be stood for a moment.

The first monthly dance at the pavilion on the archery ground was fixed for the Wednesday in the third week of July. The ballot was to take place at the Trevor Arms, on the day before the dance, and during the time that intervened between the two meetings of the committee, very little else was discussed in Olton Priors but the com-

parative chances of the respective candidates.

Between the two meetings at the hotel,
Lady Margate's dinner-party at Coddesley
was to come off; and Mrs. Hunt, determined
not to be behind-hand in canvassing, had
asked all her set to a high tea and a carpet
dance, on purpose to talk over the coming
elections.

There had been many a tiff before now
in former years between "county" and
"counter" in the Shaleford Club; the
landed proprietors wishing to make the club
a county institution; the wealthy trades-
people, manufacturers, and professional class
wishing to keep it open to all comers, and
to have the club arrangements in their own
hands entirely.

There were a few clergy who belonged to
the club, and who were more "county" than
the landed proprietors themselves; and there

was a small sprinkling of men who had retired from the service, some naval and some military, who were always of course on the "county" side ; but the attorneys and country doctors, the bankers'-clerks, and architects, auctioneers and house-agents, though occupying different social grades to one another, were all quite out of the county circles, and had formed sets of their own which were more or less sharply defined.

Of late the unpleasantness about the paper-mills had reached a high pitch. Mrs. Hunt was a clever, determined little woman, with a very bad temper, and a great dislike to gentle-people who gave themselves airs. Giving themselves airs, meant, with Mrs. Hunt, declining the honour of Mrs. Hunt's acquaintance. The Hunts were well off and pretentious, and rather led than followed such people as the Broughtons, the Brem-ridges, and the Howards. At any rate Mrs.

Hunt was quite determined on the election of Mr. Howard and Pericles Bone, and on the blackballing of young Victor Ross.

CHAPTER IX.

THE HORNETS ADVANCE IN SKIRMISHING ORDER.

THE committee of the Shaleford Club
had met on the Tuesday. Lady
Margate had issued her invitations
for dinner for the following Thursday.

She had sent invitations to Mrs. Astor and
Miss Desmoulines and to Conrad Norton;
but the idea of receiving the latter at her
husband's table became so repulsive to her as
the time drew nearer, that she determined to
appeal in person to her persecutor to influence him to stay away.

Norton had found out the social status of every one in the neighbourhood, their means, habits, birth, and parentage, in the week during which he had remained quietly at the Trevor Arms. George Warre was a garrulous person, and eager to show off his intimate knowledge of the private lives of people above him in station. Moreover, the barmaids and ostlers at the Trevor Arms were not above a gossip, especially with so handsome a man and so good a judge of a horse as Conrad Norton. They all agreed that Mr. Norton had "a way with him" which was "mighty taking." He was chatty and pleasant, without being familiar ; and he kept his own dignity while he added to theirs.

Conrad knew the value of having the servants of a household upon his side. He was a perfect master of flattery, and knew how to administer it, and in what doses, to everybody, from a duchess to a dairymaid. His good looks and his athletic figure recommended him to the women ; his ready wit and his reputation for strength and skill in manly sports made him a favourite with the men ; and his readiness to " stand" drink and cigars to every one in his company especially marked him as " a good fellow with no nonsense about him." As the drink and cigars went down in the bill, however, there was not much likelihood that Mr. Norton would be much out of pocket by his liberality.

What he had most wished to find out, had been told him by every one within twenty-four hours of his arrival at the Trevor Arms, namely, the fortunes of the younger Brooms. He knew by this time all about the value of Buncombe as a property, the amount spent in keeping it up, the settlements made upon Mrs. Broom, and the probable inheritances of Plantagenet and

Genista. Mr. Broom, in his usual bombastic manner, had taken care to let every one know his intentions about his children. " My daughter, sir, will have twenty thousand pounds on her wedding-day, and thirty thousand more when I am in my grave." This had been the way in which Mr. Broom had been accustomed to advertise Genista's charms. " My son will have Buncombe and plenty to keep it up with," had been the father's way of " cracking up" his son. This was tantamount to saying that Planty would eventually have ten thousand a year; for every one knew that Buncombe, in itself, was worthless, or worse than worthless, as an investment. The land had been part of Mambury Common, while every tree that grew on it had been planted by Mr. Broom, and, as Mr. Howard constantly affirmed, " Trees ran into money."

Norton was satisfied, therefore, that the

Brooms' fortune must be something very considerable.

He was getting very tired of the vagabond life he had hitherto led. Latterly, too, its dangers had been too great even for his adventurous spirit. The confidences of George Warre in London had first suggested to him the possibility of doing a good thing for himself in the marriage market, and the more he dwelt on that possibility, the more did it take shape and form in the person of Genista Broom.

He had never seen the girl, certainly, but that was a matter of no importance. If a woman had enough money, and was willing to bestow it and herself upon him, she might have a squint and a humpback for aught he cared.

Other possibilities had presented themselves to him, since he had known of his immediate proximity to Lord and Lady

Margate; but his designs in that quarter were at present vague and hazy, and would have to depend upon his success or the reverse in the matter of Genista Broom.

Whether Plantagenet should be made to marry Mrs. Astor or Élise, or get out of matrimony by payment of a substantial sum, was still in the womb of futurity. Sufficient unto the day was the plot thereof.

It was obvious to Conrad Norton that a too great intimacy with the *soi-disant* widow and her sister would imperil both schemes; and he had therefore made up his mind not to be seen much with them in public, nor to allow people to think it necessary to ask the three to their houses together.

He was also anxious to avoid exciting any suspicion in Lord Margate's mind that he had been a man who had known anything of that part of Lady Margate's career which had been consigned to oblivion.

When Lady Margate, therefore, met him in Olton Priors the day before the dinner-party at Coddesley, she was agreeably surprised to find how readily he fell in with her desire that he should find some excuse for absenting himself on the following day.

When Conrad had nothing to gain by being disagreeable, he was always charming. To be an attractive man was as natural to him as to be a villain. With a good digestion and a keen sense of the ridiculous, who would be a bear from choice ?

"We said, 'Silence for silence,'" said she ; " but that is no reason we should haggle over a civility, or even a kindness. It is known that you have been invited to Coddesley ; is not that enough for your purpose, whatever it may be, without making me a tool for my husband's degradation ?"

"I never intrude my company where it is not wanted," he had replied, "unless I have something to gain by the intrusion. If you do not want me at Coddesley, I am quite willing to stay away. I will send you a note to-morrow, which will settle that matter. I should like to go to the dance next Wednesday, at the pavilion. I suppose you can send me a ticket for that?"

"Certainly," said she, immensely relieved that he would not accept Lord Margate's hospitality. "Shall you want tickets for your friends as well?"

"If they cannot get them elsewhere, it would be a kindness," he answered. "But, to tell you the truth, I do not want my name coupled with theirs; so, if they are introduced by some other member, I shall be all the better pleased. Mrs. Astor is a friend to whom, years ago, I was under obligations, and, as a friend, I like her; but I do not

wish to be put down as her ' *cher ami*,' nor
have I any views with regard to her sister.
By the way, do you think Miss Desmoulines
handsome ?"

" Very ; but I do not like her face, all the
same. Her style is one men would admire
far more than women. She has money, has
she not ?"

" Not much ; the widow is the rich one.
She is a great catch for a penniless man.
The Desmoulines, you know, are of the old
French *noblesse*."

" Really ! There is a very un-English
look about both of them, certainly ; but they
speak English perfectly."

" Oh, yes ; they have lived in England all
their lives. The father was a real old aristocrat. I knew him well. The mother was
dead before I made the acquaintance of the
family ; but I believe she was some German
baroness in her own right. Not that that is

much, of course; but still, the Desmoulines are people of good family, and thoroughly well connected."

Then Lady Margate had gone on to Buncombe to call on the Brooms, and all she had heard from Norton was duly handed on to Mrs. Broom and her daughter. The Buncombe appetite for " swells " being insatiable, Mrs. Broom made up her mind there and then to call on Mrs. Astor, and learn something of the manners of " the old French *noblesse.*"

" You will meet them at our house to-morrow night," Lady Margate had said. " They are certainly very distinguished-looking people."

When Lady Margate had taken her departure, Mrs. Broom had thought over all she had been told. If Diana Trevor did not take Planty's fancy, or was not to be had for a daughter-in-law, how would the wealthy

widow or her handsome sister do for her son ?
Whatever happened, Planty must marry ;
Mrs. Broom had made up her mind on that
point. Mrs. Broom was not a straightlaced
woman by any means ; but the stories that
continued to reach her about her son's gal-
lantries in the neighbourhood, were getting
serious, to say nothing of their being disre-
putable.

CHAPTER X

THE dinner-party at Coddesley was given for the Trevors; but other interests had entered into the invitations.

Captain Norman was sincere enough in his admiration and liking for Victor Ross, and he was glad to meet in him an old school-fellow and a man who was companionable and a gentleman; but Victor's invitation to dine at Coddesley was but a stepping-stone

to Captain Norman's further views about the
Rosses.

Eva Ross had struck Captain Norman as
being one of the most beautiful women he had
ever seen ; and, in his short interview with
her at Miss Priscilla's garden-party, **he had**
declared to himself **that** her simple modesty
and dignity were beyond measure attractive.
Her repose of manner **was,** in Captain Norman's eyes, perhaps the greatest charm **of all.**
He abhorred noisy **women, fussy,** giggling
creatures, who laughed in season and out of
season, who mistook gesticulation for vivacity,
and bluntness for absence of affectation. It
was said **of** him, banteringly, **by** his friends,
that he would never marry till he was deaf,
so great a value **did** he place on repose of
manner, noiselessness of motion, and delicacy
of touch. Once, when Lady Margate had
laughingly asked him when he meant to take
a wife, he had briskly replied :

" When I meet a woman who can stand by a fireplace without bringing down the fire-irons with a crash."

Lady Margate was really anxious he should marry Genista Broom. Perhaps the fact that in that case the mother of the future heir would be no better born than herself, had something to do with Lady Margate's efforts at match-making; but she also felt that money was sorely needed to build up the fortunes of the house of Margate, and money Genista Broom would certainly have. Genista, however, as has been said, was not only plain but awkward. She upset something at table, as a rule ; she was as likely as not to break anything she touched. She had a habit of tripping herself up in her walk, and she put coals on the fire like a collier emptying a sack into the cellar. " Were she as beautiful as Venus, she would have no charms for me," Charlie Norman had once said to his sister-in-law, when she had been treating him to a catalogue of Genista's virtues, in support of her match-making views.

When Lord Margate had said, one day, to his brother, about Diana Trevor, " That's the girl for you, my boy—pretty, high-bred, well-born, and vivacious," Charlie had only re-marked that he had no fancy for a pea on a drum; that a woman who could not sit still for three seconds together, was as great a nuisance as a cockatoo ; and his remark had somewhat damped Lord Margate's hopes of a sister-in-law in Diana Trevor.

But, in Eva Ross, Charlie Norman had discovered that charm, which to him was above all others. Since Miss Priscilla's garden-party he had been almost daily at the Priory, ostensibly to play pyramids with Mr. Trevor, but really because Eva was now Diana's constant companion, while

her father and Victor were in Olton
Priors.

Lord Margate thought that his brother
was smitten with Diana's charms, and would
wink at his wife knowingly and triumph-
antly when Charlie spoke of "having his
revenge at pyramids" from Mr. Trevor,
almost every afternoon; but Diana was not
the attraction.

Not only was Eva a superb woman so far
as figure went, but her refinement of manner
equalled her grace of movement. She was
dignified without being a prude, retiring
without being shy. For all her reserve, she
was never uninteresting or inane. Her voice
was low-pitched and melodious; her gait
swift and noiseless, and queen-like; and she
seemed to know, by intuition, her distance
from everything with which she was likely to
come in contact.

A woman such as this had always been

Charlie Norman's ideal. As, day after day, he met Eva at the Priory, he more and more experienced the merging of the ideal into the real, of a poetic phantom into a beloved woman.

Norman felt, and rightly, that his brother would dislike such an alliance for the future earl; and perhaps Lady Margate might decline to call on Eva, if he allowed the truth to be suspected before the acquaintance between the families was an accomplished fact. Therefore he had piled all his admiration on to Victor, and had said no word of Eva, as yet, in discussing the Rosses' claims to social consideration.

If Lady Margate once received the brother as a guest at her own table, she could hardly refuse to call upon the sister afterwards, and Captain Norman was a man of a patient disposition, who was quite content to wait his opportunity.

Besides Victor Ross and the Trevors, there came to Coddesley that evening Miss Priscilla, who, escorted by the faithful Beer, drove herself in her own donkey-carriage, as usual; all the Brooms; Mrs. Astor and Miss Desmoulines; Dr. Grain, whose wife was an invalid, and never went into society; the Lanes of Pegwell, and the Fullers of Queen's Shaleton; the Careys of Shalebourne Manor, and the Pryce-Tynkers of Pegwell Barn. It was a large dinner-party, comprising all the *élite* of the immediate neighbourhood. Some of them, indeed, were not intimate at Coddesley, and had not even called on the Brooms; but as the party was given to the Trevors, such people as were of the best position in the neighbourhood had to be asked to meet them.

Lord and Lady Margate had had a loving little disagreement as to whom Charlie should take in to dinner, which ended in his taking Diana Trevor, and being placed next to Genista Broom on the other side, an arrangement which made the Captain, who knew very well what was being proposed for him, laugh immoderately in his sleeve.

On the other side of Diana sat Victor Ross, and next to him again, Mrs. Astor; while immediately opposite them were Planty Broom and Miss Desmoulines.

As soon as Lady Margate knew that Conrad Norton would not be at the dinner, she had asked the curate to fill the vacant place, which resulted in Mr. Channing being next Genista Broom.

Conrad Norton had said nothing, at "The Willows," of his decision not to be present at the dinner-party. Lady Margate had casually said that he had excused himself on the plea of indisposition, and that was all that transpired about the matter.

Captain Norman, between two stools,

came to the ground, at any rate as far as
conversation was concerned.   He liked
Genista Broom, and he pitied her; but he
knew that she liked the curate, and would
much rather discuss vestments with the
reverend gentleman than country gossip with
himself.   Therefore, at first he was disposed
to address himself entirely to Diana, who, on
her part, showed a partiality for conversation
on her other side, in a manner which was
certainly more marked than polite.

Being thus left in the lurch, he heard
various scraps of conversation between
Planty Broom and Miss Desmoulines, which
certainly did credit to the young lady's
powers of invention; but, at the time, Captain Norman supposed Élise to be a person
who told the truth, and her remarks made
him curious to see Mr. Conrad Norton.

" I had expected to meet Mr. Norton to-
night," Captain Norman heard Plantagenet

say. " I believe he is an old friend of yours, Miss Desmoulines ?"

" I have known him ever since I was as high as this table," she answered.

" He seems to have become a great favourite already at the Trevor Arms," said Planty; " no one can say enough good of him."

" I am sure he deserves it all," answered Élise, who had found her opportunity. " He is a wonderful man ; most men who had been made so much of in society as Mr. Norton would have been spoilt by it. But he is always the same, so generous, so manly, and so unaffected. *You* cannot fail to like him. He is just the sort of man you would get on with."

" Indeed !" said Planty, pleased with the implied compliment from lips so ripe and red. " What makes you think so ?"

" Conrad Norton has brains, and a strong will as well as a fastidious taste," she answered.

" In the short time I have known you, I have discerned the brains and the strength of will; and I have heard so much of your good taste that I think I may take that for granted."

Planty Broom beamed with gratified vanity; and Captain Norman nearly choked with suppressed laughter as he watched the fun from the other side of the table.

Just then Diana vouchsafed some attention to Captain Norman, but she speedily got round again to her right-hand companion, and Norman heard more scraps of Élise Desmoulines' remarks.

" You describe quite a hero of romance," he heard Planty say. " How much I should like to see this ' Admirable Crichton.' Is he good-looking too ?"

" Hum ! by those who admire dark men I suppose he would be considered so," said Élise, thinking of Planty's fair hair and straw-coloured moustache. " For my part, I never

think a dark man worth looking at ; so perhaps I am not a fair judge of Mr. Norton's
appearance."

This time Captain Norman let his wine go
the wrong way in his efforts to avoid laughing.
He choked audibly, but the first words he
heard on his recovery were from Planty
Broom once more :

"What sort of looking man is he ?" asked
Planty.

"I am such a bad hand at descriptions,"
answered Élise ; "but he is extraordinarily
like the gentleman opposite."

"What, the man who choked just now ?"
said Planty. "Oh ! that is Lord Margate's
brother !"

"Well ! they are alike, and they are not,"
continued Élise, looking over at Captain Norman, whose eyes were fixed on his plate.
"There is that sort of likeness that one calls
a family likeness—a likeness in feature and

colouring, but not in expression. Mr. Norton's eyes are black, while I should have said Captain Norman's were brown."

"But there is no connection between Mr. Norton and Norman, is there?" asked Planty.

"Oh! dear no; none that I ever heard of. Mr. Norton is French, I believe, on the mother's side; I have heard that his mother was a daughter of the celebrated old Duc de Vaurien. My father used to tell me strange stories of the old aristocrat. The Vaurien family were quite in the court set, you know, in the time of the 'Grand Monarque.'"

"Oh! indeed," said Planty, who was not acquainted with French history, and did not know the difference between the "Grand Monarque" and the Emperor of Morocco. "I hear you are a daughter of France too, Miss Desmoulines."

"On my father's side, yes," said Élise, unblushingly; "but we belonged to the 'Faubourg St. Germain' sets, you know; and, of course, since the Revolution we have had to rough it in exile, though, I am glad to say, not quite in destitution."

Planty made a note of "Faubourg St. Germain sets," for future inquiry, and looked it out in Genista's French Dictionary when he got home, without gaining much knowledge thereby. He quite understood, however, that the term meant something very aristocratic, and his interest increased in the stockbroker's daughter from that hour.

"You are French, too, by extraction, I presume," continued Élise presently. "Your ancestors must have been royal when ours were but millers."

Planty Broom, not being acquainted with the French language, did not follow the last part of Élise's remark, but he took the bait about royalty quite readily.

"The Herald's Office says that I am a direct

descendant of Geoffrey Plantagenet," said he, pompously, "but I fancy we Brooms have been English for a good many centuries."

Planty had been told of his great-grand-father, who had emigrated at his country's expense to Botany Bay, and though he was a fairly good liar when he had got his tongue in, preferred other topics at the present moment to a detailed review of his ancestors.

" I hope you are going to the dance at the Pavilion on Wednesday," he said, by way of changing the conversation.

" We should like to, but we have not been asked," answered Élise.

" My mother will be delighted to send you tickets, I am sure," said Planty. " I will bring them to 'The Willows' to-morrow, if you will allow me."

Then Diana had again given Captain Norman a turn, and this time she seemed to have felt some compunction for her former neglect, for she kept him engaged till the ladies left the dining-room.

Diana was sprightly and vivacious and satirical, but her conversation made no impression on Captain Norman. He was thinking of Eva Ross.

CHAPTER XI.

BEHIND THE VEIL.

RS. ASTOR certainly had not en-
joyed herself. She had been taken
with Victor at first sight, it is true.
She admired the colossal proportions of the
man, his golden beard, and his keen blue
eyes; but she found him very bad company
indeed, and freely forgave him for giving
to Diana the somewhat awkward attempts at
making conversation with which he had at
first honoured her.

Victor was not a lady's man, to begin with;

and he was not a man who knew much of London-life scandals or amusements. Mrs. Astor's fascinations were entirely thrown away upon him while Diana was by; and as she fairly owned she knew nothing and cared less about field sports and country pursuits generally, he had found the task of entertainment almost hopeless.

Old Mr. Pryce-Tynker, on Mrs. Astor's other side, was certainly not an improvement on Victor Ross. He had lost most of his teeth. He mumbled his food. He talked with his mouth full; and, worst of all, he was a married man. Mrs. Astor could forgive much in the trousered sex, but matrimony was a bar to all further interest on her part. Élise seemed to be making good the running with Mr. Plantagenet Broom. Mrs. Astor was accustomed to playing second fiddle to Élise, and she did not envy her Planty Broom Boys with straw-coloured moustaches were not in Mrs. Astor's line; and, to Mrs. Astor, Planty Broom seemed scarcely more than a boy. So long, however, as he was over twenty-one, that was all that mattered to Élise. Still the dinner was none the less dull to Mrs. Astor. She was not sorry when Lady Margate gave the signal for leaving the gentlemen to their wine, though she scarcely knew to what purpose she could put her talents in a roomful of women.

At first it certainly did seem as though she had stepped from the frying-pan into the fire. Both she and her sister were entire strangers to the society of Sandshire. Élise, however, had fastened on Genista Broom, to whom she was expressing her delight in having met so charming a man as Plantagenet.

Genista, being plain and awkward, was the more proud of her smart, good-looking brother, and drank in his praises with avidity. She, too, heard all about the Duc de Vaurien, the Faubourg St. Germain, and the "Grand Monarque," and was duly dazzled by Élise's description of Conrad Norton's good looks, good birth, and good breeding.

But it was dull, very dull for Mrs. Astor. She had gone to a table on which were a pile of photographs of Switzerland and the Rhine, and as she slowly turned them over, she heard a mingled hum of women's voices discussing servants and babies, soothing syrups, and the price of velvet, with scraps of the peerage and "who's who," without which no drawing-room conversation would seem to be complete.

At last Miss Priscilla noticed that Mrs. Astor was being neglected. She forsook the old lady with whom she had been discussing list tippets and linsey-woolsey petticoats, to find out if Mrs. Astor took any interest in the social condition of the working-classes.

Poor Mrs. Astor! Her widow's cap, and her piquant but pensive face, had given Miss Priscilla the idea that charity in some form must be a sympathetic topic. There is nothing so healing to a wounded heart as daily thought and work for others. Would Mrs. Astor undertake a district in the parish? Poor Mrs. Golightly was delicate, and found her duties too much for her. Perhaps Miss Desmoulines would help in the boys' night-school. A mother's-meeting was to be held in the school-room the following week; Miss Priscilla hoped Mrs. Astor would accompany her!

Mrs. Astor determined on going into half-mourning next day; weeds might be becoming, but they had their disadvantages!

Then the gentlemen came in, and matters improved. Captain Norman singled her out, paid her great attention, talked on subjects she could understand and appreciate, gave her opportunities of showing off her knowledge of a world outside mothers'-meetings and clothing-clubs, and altogether proved a very charming companion.

When Miss Priscilla went out to dinner, she waited for nobody to make a homeward move. Barker thought early hours good for Miss Priscilla, and the old lady was as obedient now as when she had been a child. So, at eleven o'clock, Miss Priscilla was heard to inquire if "her Jehu" had come round. Lord Margate stared, not being sufficiently acquainted with Miss Priscilla's peculiarities of diction; but on its being explained to him that Miss Priscilla's "Jehu" was no other than the worthy Beer, whose extremely slow pace in driving had earned him the name in satire, he made the requisite inquiries.

Miss Priscilla's departure was a sign for general dispersion. The Trevors offered Victor a place in their carriage as far as the Priory, on his way to Black Rock, which saved him two miles' walk, and which he was only too glad to accept; while the curate, after taking leave of Genista with a lingering pressure, intended to convey unutterable things, accepted a lift in Dr. Grain's olive-green pill-box.

On leaving Coddesley, Mrs. Astor found her sister in high spirits. Planty Broom had escorted Élise to the fly, and Élise had rewarded him with one such flash from her dark eyes as had sent the arrow straight home. Planty was made of inflammable stuff; Élise's meretricious charms had already warmed him. She had, too, tickled his vanity, and fostered his good opinion of himself in many ways.

"Among all the idiotic noodles of my

acquaintance," said Élise to her sister, as she settled herself back in the uncomfortable fly, "I give that young Broom-sprig the palm. Hopkins and Jenkyns were swell-mobsmen in sagacity to this young prig. He is vain enough to swallow any bait, hook and all, so long as one flatters his self-esteem."

"You think, then, he will be better for a breach of promise than a wedding-ring?" asked her sister rather coldly, for she had felt eclipsed by Élise rather too obviously that evening.

"I don't say that. The ring would be worth ten thousand a year, so Con tells me; while one could hardly hope for more than five thousand down, even from a scion of the House of Anjou, for a breach of promise. No; I think, if the promise to marry can be brought to a fulfilment, the sauce would make the goose sufficiently savoury."

"He is a good-looking youth, and well

set-up," said Mrs. Astor; "a great improvement on the rest of his family, I should say, judging merely by appearances."

"Well! the father is a pompous old snob, and that awkward girl seems quite a nonentity in the family; but the mother has brains, and would be quite unscrupulous, I fancy, as to any means she might employ to secure her ends."

Mrs. Astor laughed. "She is not singular," she said; "we know of others who can be equally unscrupulous."

"How did you get on with that young giant who took you in to dinner?" asked Élise. "That is what I call a proper man. He would be a model for a Hercules to any sculptor."

"Very likely," rejoined Mrs. Astor. "For me, I am not fond of louts. He is very handsome certainly, but he has not a word to say for himself. I dare say felling timber in his shirt-sleeves he looks very picturesque, and one could fancy him appearing to advantage as a Roman Gladiator, but he is a ponderous and placid creature and not at all in my line."

"So it seemed," said Élise sharply, "nor you in his, to judge by the small amount of attention he paid you. He seems smitten with that pert little minx, Miss Trevor. That girl is quite odious! don't you think so?"

"I have had no opportunity of judging," said Mrs. Astor, who, surprised by her sister's words and manner, rapidly put two and two together, and thought it was a great pity she and Élise had not been able to change places. Then, after a pause, she added: "I do not think the Trevor girl would condescend to your yellow-haired hero; he is only a timber-merchant, and his father was the son of the village carpenter here in Olton Priors."

Élise did not answer. She was thinking how different her life might have been if such a one as this Victor Ross had been thrown in her path years ago, instead of the effeminate striplings whom she had at once encouraged and despised. Heartless and designing as Élise Desmoulines was, she was a woman still, not an unsexed fiend. She had never loved, therefore her heart was hard as a nether mill-stone, but she had had her dreams, like another, of an ideal hero who should command her heart and her; only she had never met him in the flesh— till now! No creature on this earth is wholly bad. In the most degraded souls there glimmers, though obscured by sin and callousness, some flickering spark of light. The emotion that touched Élise as she lay back in the darkness was not love, nor was it shame, but still it was one that was akin to both. She was a woman of strong passions, this stockbroker's daughter — all the stronger for never having been frittered away on countless loves. Her whole physique suggested redundant vigour and latent force. The day must come when passion would assert its sway, and burst the barriers of banked-up nature. Passion, in such a woman as Élise, would be a terrible power. If returned, it might transform her into an angel of light; but if not, her own fire would consume her, and, like another Semele, she would perish in the flame of her own creation.

She was roused from her reverie by her sister asking her if she saw any likeness in Captain Norman to any one they knew.

"He is built in the same mould as Con," said Élise in reply. "I was greatly struck by the resemblance at first sight, but it wears off when Captain Norman speaks. Con is the handsomer of the two, to my thinking ; at any rate he has a much greater spice of the devil about him. Captain Norman, after Con, is like claret after champagne."

" He is tame by comparison," assented Mrs. Astor; "still he is very handsome and very agreeable. I wonder what freak made Con stay away. He is never ill, and I thought he particularly wanted to stand well with Lady Margate."

" I dare say he has not lost in her lady-ship's good graces by absenting himself," said her sister. " There is more than meets the eye in this move of Mr. Conrad Norton's, my dear; you may take my word for that. I dare say, if the truth were known, our friend Con knows a good deal about Lady Margate which Sandshire must not hear or even suspect."

" Do you think so !" said Mrs. Astor, suddenly becoming animated. " She does not give me the impression of—of—you know what I mean."

"We do not all carry our hearts on our sleeves, Anne, nor our characters either, for the matter of that; Lady Margate seems a very devoted little wife now, at all events; but I think Con knows more about her than he chooses to tell us, all the same."

Then Mrs. Astor was silent. She tried to persuade herself that she was only a very unhappy woman, who had been forced into marriage with a decrepit old man by the hardness of fate, and she viewed her own lapse from virtue very leniently from a moral point of view. She also had tried to persuade herself that she liked the excitement of hunting in couples with Conrad Norton, merely for the excitement's sake, and that it would have been quite as pleasant with any Tom, Dick, or Harry of her acquaintance who was as good company and as keen-witted as Conrad Norton. But even the suggestion that Lady Margate might once have been dear to Conrad caused her a jealous pang. She had been pleased with Captain Norman, Why? because she had been reminded of Conrad while she had conversed with a man who was somewhat like him. Mrs. Astor had loved before; but that was years ago; and the man she had so loved was dead. She was not like Élise. She was not so strong a character, though more feminine. But she too was suffering from the shafts of passion, though she had not yet recognised the nature of the poison in her veins.

CHAPTER XII.

THE opposition gathered in full force at the large white house adjoining the paper-mills, where the Hunts lived in plenty and comfort, on the same night as Lady Margate gave her dinner-party.

The opposition comprised the "counter" set, the professional set, and big townspeople of Olton Priors. There were Bremridge, the old attorney, and his wife and daughters, and Broughton, the junior partner, who had once been Bremridge's office clerk, and his wife and her sister, Miss Spink. There were Boodle the station-master, and Pericles Bone; the Howards, and Mr. Moggs, the Potteries' manager, from Bossy-Compton; there were an Olton Priors schoolmaster, a Mr. Timothy Fluke, who kept an academy for young gentlemen, and his maiden sister, Miss Keziah Fluke; also two young clerks from Catspar's Bank. Fortunately the Misses Bremridge were legion, otherwise Mrs. Hunt would have had a superabundance of men.

There was yet another distinct set which the "counter" affected to look down upon, and which also looked down upon the "counter," a set which may best be described as one of substantial yeomen. Sandshire was emphatically an agricultural county, a corn-growing county, and some of its well-to-do farmers were persons of considerable importance, even

though they held no county position whatever.   This set—though formed for the most
part of uneducated countrymen, men who
dined in their kitchens and smoked their
pipes on the cosy settle—had, nevertheless, a
much stronger leaning towards " county "
than " counter."   The young men of this
class · met the " county " at the meet, were
sometimes asked by Lord Margate and others
to have a day's shooting over their preserves,
and were companions to gentlemen in half a
hundred ways in which young men of the
" counter " set were not.

   To this class had the ancestors of both
Ross and Warre belonged, and to this class
George Warre belonged still, while, through
the Leslie connection, the Rosses had stepped
nearer to " county " circles.   George Warre
was a mighty favourite with all the young
Sandshire yeomen, for, with the exception of
Victor Ross, there was not a man in the

county could ride straighter, or wrestle better, or run up a better score at the wickets, than young George Warre.

Camilla Howard had asked Mrs. Hunt to invite George Warre, for Camilla knew a proper man when she saw one, and considered the stalwart young fellow worth twenty bankers' clerks or country doctors; but Mrs. Hunt had turned up her nose at the idea of a publican's son, even though her own brother was station-master at Shalemouth. Also Mrs. Hunt had another reason for not wishing to include George Warre in her list of invitations. Her brother had let her into his heart's secret, which was his passion for Camilla Howard, and Mr. Boodle did not contrast favourably with George Warre. Mr. Boodle's name was Septimus; he was knock-kneed, and of a bilious complexion. He was a damp young man, too, very damp, and he wore flannel shirts with a linen "dickey."

Camilla Howard did not reciprocate Mr. Boodle's passion.

First of all there was a high tea in Mrs. Hunt's best parlour—a regular sit down affair, with abundance of fish, flesh, and fowl, and wine and beer for those that liked them. There were junkets and squab-pies, and other Sandshire dishes, cunningly made by Mrs. Hunt herself. Mrs. Howard was by birth a Sandshire woman, and she dearly loved Mrs. Hunt's squab-pies. Mrs. Hunt allowed that Mrs. Rhodes, the Olton Priors confectioner, made the best " parliament," but she made her own potato-cakes, and vowed they were greatly superior to those of Mrs. Rhodes.

After tea, Mrs. Hunt asked Pericles Bone for a comic song, to the great delight of old Mr. Howard, who listened with rapt attention to " The little wee Dawg," and " As I vas a vollacking down the Street," two compositions of an advanced musical order which gave boundless gratification to Boodle and to Catspar's clerks.

Then the tables were cleared away, and they had a dance, not such a dance as was usual at the Pavilion certainly, but still a dance, for at the Pavilion people who could not dance in such a manner as was usual in polite society, sat out; but at Mrs. Hunt's everybody danced, even old Howard and his wife and Mr. Bremridge, who was seventy if he was an hour. There was a good deal of twirling in the quadrilles, and galloping round at intervals, and pirouetting and bowing to partners, which would have probably astonished Lady Adela Trevor; but then Lady Adela was not acquainted with the muse of dancing as seen at Cremorne or the "Hall by the Sea." There was a good deal of brisk polking, and a schottisch and a varsoviana, and several country dances of the romp order, no particular steps or figures, but plenty of

waist business, and as many twirls as would
not have disgraced a dancing dervish.

The Misses Bremridge got very giddy and
the old people very blown, especially Mrs.
Howard, who had undertaken the consump-
tion of nearly a whole squab-pie ; but most
of them concurred in the opinion that Mrs.
Hunt's carpet dance was most enjoyable.

CHAPTER XIII.

WHEN the Howards arrived at home, the sisters arrayed themselves in their *peignoirs* in Camilla's bedroom, and proceeded to hair-brushing and confidence.

Camilla had been unusually silent on the drive home, and Penelope—or, as she was called by her own people, "Penny"—felt sure that something more than ordinary had befallen her sister.

The girls were both handsome, big, well-developed women, with strongly marked features and a high colour; women who, ten years later, would in all probability be coarse and masculine looking; but as yet the worst that could be said of them was that they were almost unbecomingly healthy.

Camilla was the larger and darker woman of the two, and in character the bolder and the more enterprising.

Very handsome she looked with her masses of dark hair tumbling over her ample shoulders; but her expression was troubled, more scornful than sad, and she threw herself into a low arm-chair with a deep sigh of vexation and discontent.

"When is this awful kind of life to cease?" she asked, as Penelope threw herself into a companion chair. "I loathe myself every time I enter the society of such people as those Hunts."

"My dear, what can we expect?" replied

Penelope, who was less discontented and more of a philosopher than her sister. "Papa is very good to us, and mamma is the best-intentioned woman living ; but who would have them as guests at any good house in the neighbourhood ?"

"Oh ! I do not mean to complain of the dear old dad," said Camilla, "nor of our mother either. They are as good as gold, and as unselfish as—anything ; but the society they mix with, and compel us to mix with, is perfectly intolerable. I sometimes feel as if I could stand it no longer."

"What can we do ? The county people won't know us, and I am sure I don't wonder. Yet there must be heaps of girls nowadays who suffer tortures from the vulgarity of their parents, and who yet manage to pull through, and marry into fair positions after all."

"I am not sure that I want to know the

'county' sets," said Camilla musingly. "The womenkind are so stuck-up, and gentlemen are so insipid!"

"My dear Camilla," exclaimed her sister, horrified, "what do you mean by 'gentlemen are so insipid?'"

"Just what I say," answered Camilla sharply; "all the so-called swells hereabouts—the men I mean—are lanky, lackadaisical mannikins, without an ounce of muscle about them. I do like a man to be a man, not a padded whipping-post or a tailor's dummy. Look at those Lanes and the young Pryce-Tynkers. A rag doll has more shape than any of them, and I do believe, as far as strength goes, I could throw any one of them into the middle of next week."

"They are effeminate-looking, certainly, but I think you have picked out an exceptionally poor lot as specimens of the "county" men. Captain Norman is as strong a man as one would wish to see. I am sure there is nothing effeminate about him."

"No! not effeminate exactly," assented Camilla, "but he is too much of the claret-and-water sort for my taste; a sort of man, I should think, who would ask for a kiss before he took it, and then bestow it on some one's 'pure uplifted brow.'"

"You would be the last person to allow a man to take a liberty with you, Camilla."

"It would depend upon who took the liberty, Penny."

"My dear, you had better go out to Australia, to Jane" (Jane was the married sister who lived in the Bush), "I dare say there are plenty of brawny muscular heroes out there who will kiss you whether you like it or not. For my part I prefer to be asked first."

" And within call of a policeman if you choose to refuse," added Camilla, laughing. " Well, I don't think I shall go in search of a bush-ranger, but still gentlemen are so very insipid."

" If you talk such nonsense, Camilla, I shall go to bed."

" No! don't do that, Penny, I have got something to tell you — something really spicey, only to me it was beyond a joke, it nearly made me sick."

" Which! the squab-pie or the potato-cake ?"

" Neither, it was Septimus Boodle."

" What, did he kiss you ?"

" *He* kiss me !" cried Camilla, tossing back her mane of hair with intense disgust, " he would have soon found himself in the grate if he had tried that. No! he did not ask me to kiss him, he asked me to marry him !"

" Camilla !" exclaimed her sister, " you don't really mean it !"

" I do though," said Camilla, " that sickly kangaroo of a creature actually had the audacity to ask me to be his wife. Ugh !" and Camilla shuddered.

" And a station-master too !" said Penelope ; " we shall be supposed to be fair game for the guards and porters next, I suppose."

" They would not be half so bad," said Camilla, bent on teasing her sister. " The guards are fine men as a rule, and the porters are strong, even if they do smell of train-oil ; but a station-master, my dear, a wretched little putty-faced clerk, with a figure like a merry-thought, and the neck of a giraffe ! Bah ! the butcher boy would have been a cherished alternative !"

" Camilla, have you gone quite out of your

senses? How can you run on in this wild way? Mr. Boodle is not a desirable lover, I own, though I dare say he has his merits in his own sphere. A worthy young man, no doubt. I can understand your being annoyed, but I see nothing in his proposal to cause such loathing and disgust."

"My dear Penny, I felt sure the proposal was coming, before we went to the Hunts to-night, and I have been gradually sickening over it all day. As long as a man like Boodle keeps his distance, wears gloves when he shakes hands, and confines himself to the merest conventionalities, one can put up with his being an under-bred little snobling, and a repulsive specimen of humanity, but it is quite another thing when such a man makes love to one. All the men one meets at the Hunts are, to my thinking, repulsive, but none of them so much so as Boodle."

Penelope grew very red, but Camilla was

now brushing her long hair, and did not observe it.

"What did you say to him, Camilla?" said Penny presently.

"Oh! I said it was quite out of the question, of course, that I was very sorry if I had unintentionally given him any encouragement, but that such an idea had never entered my head, and so on; then he asked me if I would not take time to think of it, and I said I was quite, *quite* sure that it could never be. Why! Penny, I absolutely loathe the sight of the man!"

"Well, my dear, I am not standing up for him, and I should have been very sorry indeed, if you had given him any other answer. But, Mr. Boodle's offer apart, we are neither of us in the first flush of youth, and I do wish sometimes we saw a little more society. I am not the woman to throw myself at a man's head, but I should be sorry to live and die an old maid."

" How about the curate, Penny?" said Camilla, looking sly.

" I like him very much, very much indeed," said Penelope gravely; "but I would never marry him. I respect him more than I can say, but I could never love him, nor have I ever seen that he cares one farthing about me."

" Then I suppose it is Genista," said Camilla.

" I think so," said Penelope, "but I am very sorry for the poor man; I do not think Genista quite knows what love means She is a very passionless woman apparently, and even if she encouraged him, I am certain the Brooms would never give their consent."

" Oh! Genista's heart will wake up when the right man comes, you may be sure; but

for my part I think she does care for the
curate, though perhaps not in the way that
you or I would care for a man."

"I cannot say; Genista is so very reserved. I think Lady Margate would like
her to marry Captain Norman."

"My dear, men don't marry by order,
especially a sister-in-law's order. Besides, I
hear Captain Norman is at the Priory all
day long. He has lost no time in making up
to Miss Trevor."

"That would be a much more suitable
match," said Penelope. "I wonder whether
papa will be elected to the Shaleford Club.
It would make all the difference in the world
to us girls."

"I do not think we have many enemies,
even if we have but few friends," said
Camilla. "I dare say we shall pull through
all right. By the way, what a dead set
there is against those Rosses!"

"Jealousy, mere jealousy," said the younger sister. "Mr. Ross's marriage with Miss Leslie gave him a lift from the yeoman class into a quasi-county set; that is a sort of thing such people as the Hunts and the Broughtons never forgive."

"I wish we knew them. Young Ross is something like a man, and Miss Ross is out-and-out the finest girl near here. Perhaps if we are all elected on Wednesday, we shall at last make their acquaintance."

"The Brooms have not called on them, and do not mean to," said Penelope; "Planty Broom cannot bear Victor Ross."

"I did not know they were acquainted."

"They have met out hunting, and there was some unpleasantness last winter between them. I do not know the circumstances."

"At any rate, it would be the Rosses' place to call on the Brooms. Because old Broom has built Buncombe, he seems to think he can ride rough-shod over the whole county."

" How should you vote, if we already belonged to the club ?"

" For the Rosses, of course."

" Why ?"

Camilla grew red and hesitated.

" Why ! Oh ! because I like to look at fine specimens of humanity, I suppose. The Rosses are ornaments to every party they attend."

" Oh ! I thought perhaps you had been taking a lesson in hero-worship from George Warre !"

Camilla grew scarlet, but made no reply.

" Seriously, Camilla, you should not let that young Warre pay you so much attention."

" Why not ?"

" Why not ! Because, of course, you would never dream of marrying a publican's son ; and it is cruel to give him false hopes."

"George Warre is worth a dozen Boodles!" exclaimed Camilla excitedly. "In fact, it is an insult to him to mention his name in the same breath with the men we met at the Hunts' to-night."

"My dear Camilla!"

"He is not refined," continued Camilla, "and I suppose most people would say he was ugly; "but he is a man, every inch of him—a great, strong, sturdy man, and as bold as a lion!"

"You are quite right. He is not refined —far from it; and he is ugly, with his square jaw and clean-shaven face, and throat like a young bull. I always took him for a young prize-fighter, till Miss Priscilla told me who he was."

"I like bull-necks," said Camilla, brushing her hair very hard, "and I like clean-shaven faces, and I like square jaws."

"Then you had better go to Australia, to

Jane," said Penelope. " I dare say bush-rangers will suit your fancy, and perhaps they would shave if you found them the razors.   And now I'm off to bed."

CHAPTER XIV.

WHEN a country town gives itself to the discussion of one subject, and that subject a social one, hard words are plentiful.

During the week between the preliminary committee and the day fixed for the ballot, Olton Priors had been divided into two hostile camps, while the names of the various candidates for membership of the Shaleford Club were in everybody's mouth.

Of course, there were people who meant

to vote for all the nominees; and, again, there were others who intended to exclude all if they had the power.

Dr. Grain, for instance, had openly expressed a hope that all his patients would do him a personal favour by electing his rival, Pericles Bone; and the old physician, frill and all, attended at the Trevor Arms to record his own vote in the smart surgeon's favour.

Miss Priscilla, again, would as soon have thought of contributing a blackball to anybody's detriment as of thrashing her donkeys or drowning the tortoise-shell Tom. Reticule on arm, Miss Priscilla marched down to the Trevor Arms on that important Tuesday, and voted for every one whose name was on the list.

The Brooms, on the other hand, blackballed every one except the Howards. Mrs. Broom and Planty would have blackballed even them, but **Mr.** Broom and Genista were obdurate ; so it ended in a compromise, and the Howards were neither better nor worse for the countenance of the " House of Anjou." As to the Rosses, Plantagenet said he would not stay in the club if that " great hulking woodman," as he stigmatised Victor Ross, were allowed to become a member; so Ross had four blackballs from Buncombe alone.

The talk of the election had been so incessant, the discussion so warm, and party feeling so high, that by the time the members were all assembled at the Trevor Arms, most people knew how most other people were going to vote, and a prolific crop of dragon's-teeth was sown for future harvesting.

Everybody came. From far and near for miles round every member of the Shaleford Club was eager to have a finger in the pie.

It was "County versus Counter." That was understood. The excitement was intense. Mr. Broom had been heard to declare that the meeting would be a death-blow to the club, and Mr. Broom was a person of much sagacity. The excitement had communicated itself to the whole town, even to people who had never even seen the Pavilion, and who would not have known how to draw a bow or handle a cricket-bat.

The assembly-room at the Trevor Arms was densely packed. It was a question of social life and death. Either the Shaleford Club was an exclusive club, a county club, or it was a popular gathering to which all the "ragtag and bobtail" might demand admittance.

The Lanes were there, of course—"the young men with no more shape than a rag doll," as Camilla Howard had said—and the Pryce-Tynkers, whose lack of biceps and calf had so impressed the same young lady; and the Fullers of Queen's Shaleton, and the Careys of Shalebourne Manor, and the Brooms, and the Hunts, and the Broughtons, and the Bremridges, and a score or so more families of "county" and "counter" sets, besides many of the intermediate social strata, professional men, tradesmen, and yeomen.

People greeted one another with more meaningless laughter than usual, and with visible embarrassment. It was felt that, under certain circumstances, this might be the last time "county" and "counter" would meet on speaking terms. Perhaps to-morrow the two sets might be "dead cuts."

At last, amidst breathless excitement, Mr. Broom, who had been whispering for some moments to Lady Margate, got on his legs and read out the result of the ballot.

The show of hands on the previous Tuesday was proved to be a fairly correct index of popular feeling.   Mr Trevor, Mr. Pryce-Tynker, Mr. Channing, and Mr. Herries of Applecombe Farm were elected.   The Shalemouth lot, including Mr. Hedgering, Sir Rufus MacGregor, and Septimus Boodle, were rejected.   Mrs. Hunt was furious ; but no one else much cared whether Boodle was at the Pavilion or at the bottom of the Dead Sea. Then came the real tug of war.   Mr. Moggs of Bossy-Compton and Mr. Pericles Bone were elected.   The Howards got in by the skin of their teeth, the blackballs being thirty-nine to forty-one white.

Victor Ross was not elected.

Then arose a confused hum of many voices. People got together in little knots and shook hands fussily, feeling by no means sure that Mr. Broom's declaration had been an end of the matter.

Miss Priscilla gathered her skirts together, adjusted her sunshade, grasped her parasol firmly in one hand and her reticule in the other, and made for the door.

Mrs. Hunt bowed furtively as Miss Priscilla passed, but the old lady only twitched her nose viciously in Mrs. Hunt's direction, and passed her with her chin high in the air.

George Warre was standing at the door of the Trevor Arms, very horsily dressed, talking to Mr. Conrad Norton. His clothes were so tight that they seemed to have been sewn on to him, and he tapped his high boots jauntily with his riding-whip, and wore his hat very much cocked on one side. Miss Priscilla recollected that Victor was attached to this young man, so she forgave him for looking a cross between a groom and a prize-fighter, even though she so strongly disapproved of his slangy manner. She held out her hand to him, when he raised his hat to her respectfully as she passed, and said in

Conrad Norton's hearing, "I want you to come and dine with me one evening; I am an old woman, and not very good company, but I hope you will come."

George blushed to the very roots of his close-cut hair as he stammered his delighted acceptance. Then Miss Priscilla made a little formal bow as she passed Norton, to whom she had not yet been introduced, and went up the street to her own home.

"My stars and garters!" exclaimed George Warre to Conrad, as soon as the old lady was out of hearing; "what can be the meaning of this? I shall be dining with Lord Margate next! I wonder what is up?"

"That old lady is Miss Trevor, is she not?" said Conrad.

"Yes; she holds her head mighty high in these parts, as all the Trevors always have done. If Miss Priscilla calls anywhere, the county calls; if Miss Priscilla stays away, the county stays away too. Whatever can she want me to dine there for ?"

The young fellow's face beamed with delight. He was a lusty, good-humoured, rollicking man, as strong as a young bull, and true and honest and bold; but he had never set foot in the houses of either "county" or "counter" as a guest; and to be asked to dinner by Miss Priscilla was an honour of which he felt really proud.

"He loves the Rosses," muttered Miss Priscilla, as she walked up the street. "He shall dine at my house."

Miss Priscilla walked briskly enough till she found herself within her own gates. Then she thought she was not quite so strong as she had been, and she sat down awhile on a garden seat.

How should she tell the Rosses that Victor was blackballed for the Shaleford Club ?

She got up and walked on. The donkeys were harnessed in the little carriage, and were standing at the door; but Miss Priscilla did not even pat them as she passed them by. The tortoise-shell Tom rubbed himself against Miss Priscilla's dress, in token of welcome, but the old lady took no heed. Barker stood with folded hands, ready to take the reticule and parasol, but Miss Priscilla did not seem to see her.

How should she tell the Rosses?

CHAPTER XV.

MISS PRISCILLA entered her sitting-room and shut the door. Then Barker heard the key turn in the lock. Miss Priscilla had locked herself in.

"This won't do," said Barker to herself as she heard the click of the bolt. "I wonder what on earth is up now!" Then Barker went round by the back-yard and out again into the lawn. The day was hot, and the window of the sitting-room was open. Barker made swiftly for the open casement.

There was Miss Priscilla at the old bureau, and in her hands the faded bunch of myrtle-sprays, as dry and dead as lavender picked years ago. As Barker reached the window, she saw Miss Priscilla raise the twigs to her lips, kiss them once, twice, thrice, and then fall, sobbing as if her heart would break, on the slab of the old bureau.

"Drat them sticks! I wish they was at the bottom of the sea, that I do!" said Barker with some asperity, as she crossed the room to where Miss Priscilla, her head on her hands, her hands grasping the dear dead reminders of a long past youth, leaned sobbing, and rocking herself to and fro. "Now, this sort of thing I will not have, Miss Priscilla, so it's no use your going on so." Then Barker, nearly in tears herself, lifted the grey head from the myrtle-sprays, and kissed Miss Priscilla as though she had been a child hurt by a tumble on the floor. "Now, put away them things," said Barker in a coaxing tone, as she disengaged the withered stalks from the old lady's grasp, and returned them to their own particular drawer. "Dear heart! what has happened to upset you so?" Then Barker too gave way for very sympathy, and the two old women, mistress and maid, whose hearts were as green as when they made cowslip balls in the Priory meadows, cried over each other to their hearts' content.

"It's about the Rosses, Barker," said Miss Priscilla, gulping back her tears.

"Of course it's about the Rosses," echoed Barker; "Lord love us! as if I didn't know that before ever you spoke."

"It's all that Mrs. Hunt," continued Miss Priscilla.

For a moment Barker was puzzled what tack to go on. She persevered as an echo for the present.

"Of course it's that Mrs. Hunt," she replied.

"I've tried! I am sure I've tried to be kind to all my neighbours," sobbed Miss Priscilla, "and to live in charity with all men."

"And women too, for the matter of that, I am sure you have," interrupted Barker in a tone of consolation.

"As a decent Christian woman should; and though I did think the Hunts were wrong to put up a station-master for the club, yet I went down to give my vote myself for Mr. Boodle, lest I should appear unkind."

"Yes! yes! I know you did, Miss Priscilla; but, deary me, what has this to do with the Rosses?"

"They have blackballed Victor! my Victor!" cried Miss Priscilla furiously, while her nose twitched violently in the direction of imaginary Hunts, "people who are not fit to black his shoes."

"The impudent beasts!" said Barker sympathisingly, "but what could you expect from them stuck-up manufacturers?"

"They shall never enter my doors again, never!" said Miss Priscilla, recovering her dignity in proportion as she lost her temper, and stamping her foot furiously on the floor.

"But, dear heart, there must have been more than them Hunts in it," said Barker sagaciously. "It takes a lot of them black-balls to exclude any one, don't it?"

"Of course it does. Oh! if I could only find out who has done this, not one of them should ever enter my gates again."

"Well, miss, maybe I can help you," said Barker, as oracularly as if she were standing on the Tripod in the midst of the Delphic Temple. "Me and Beer, you know, miss, do hear a many things in the town that

29—2

never reach gentlefolks' ears. One way and another things leak out, Miss Priscilla, and the whole place has been agog this week past about them dratted elections for the club."

"Yes, Barker, yes!" said Miss Priscilla eagerly; "tell me all you have heard, all."

"Well, miss, it is Beer's cousin, you know, who waits out to parties when the people has no man of their own, and it was Beer's cousin who waited at them Hunts' hop last Thursday night. Well, of course he hears the conversation, and when he hears the name of Victor Ross, he pricks up his ears, knowing how fond you are of the young man, miss; and what Beer's cousin heard, he tells Beer, and Beer tells me."

"Yes! yes! I understand; and what did he hear?"

"Well! Mrs. Hunt and Mrs. Broughton were that set against Victor Ross being

elected to the club, that they made out a
list of all the voters, and then asked every
one to put their mark who would vote against
Victor Ross. People did not like to refuse
Mrs. Hunt just as they were full of her
squab-pie and potato-cakes, specially as very
few of them knew Victor Ross to speak to,
so 'most everybody signed."

"Why should Mrs. Hunt dislike Victor?
What has he ever done to her?"

"He was proposed by Lord Margate, Miss
Priscilla."

"And seconded by me," said the old lady
haughtily.

"Of course Lord Margate's name is like
mad dogs to them Hunts," resumed Barker,
"and just because his lordship took Victor
up, therefore Mrs. Hunt must set him
down."

"I suppose there were fifty or sixty people
at Mrs. Hunt's?"

"About fifty, so Beer's cousin says; but Mrs. Hunt didn't get it all her own way, far from it. Miss Howard—the eldest one—I think she is called Camilla—heard what was going on, and when that young woman has an opinion, she is bound to express it, so they say; well! Miss Camilla, she spoke up fine for Victor Ross, and said straight out that all the men were jealous of him, and all the women were jealous of Miss Eva; then there was such a fuss, and Miss Penny took her sister's part, and stood out for the Rosses against the lot. I don't like them Howards, Miss Priscilla, as you very well know, but I will say as how they have behaved handsome about Victor Ross."

"I shall ask those Howard girls to dinner," said Miss Priscilla.

"But, miss, it was not Mrs. Hunt alone who was determined against Victor Ross. Them Brooms is worse."

"The Brooms!" exclaimed Miss Priscilla, "impossible! of course the Brooms voted for Victor. Even if they do not know the Rosses, they are intimate with Lady Margate, and they know me."

"For all that they voted against Victor," said Barker doggedly. "The footman up to Buncombe came in to tea last Sunday evening with Beer and me—for it was his Sunday out, and the young woman he is keeping company with was ill in bed, and couldn't walk with him, so he didn't know where to go—and the footman said he had heard Mr. Planty say, that if that 'hulking woodman' (that's what he called Victor, Miss Priscilla), that if that 'hulking woodman' belonged to the club, he should resign."

"Oh! Planty Broom called Victor a 'hulking woodman,' did he?" said Miss Priscilla; "very good—go on, Barker, go on."

"Well! Mr. Broom argued with Mr. Planty, and Miss Genista said it was a shame to blackball him, but Mr. Planty got into a dreadful rage, and swore they should choose between Victor and him; so at last the others had to give way, and that made four more blackballs for Victor."

Miss Priscilla went on nodding her head mechanically.

"Why should Planty Broom hate my Victor?"

"Lor', Miss Priscilla, have you never heard? Why, out hunting one day, Planty Broom cut a boy over the face with his whip, because the boy did not hold open the gate for him; and Victor chucked Planty Broom into the pond, there and then, and they have been at daggers drawn ever since."

"That will do, Barker; yes, now I think I understand. Now you may leave me for the present."

CHAPTER XVI.

HE first "grand day" of the Shaleford Club, the Wednesday so much looked forward to in Olton Priors, was a bright, sunny summer day in the early part of July.

The cricket-match was between North and South Sandshire, but the majority of the ladies did not come to look on at the match, and had reserved themselves for the picnic dinner at six o'clock, followed by the dance at eight.

Between five and six, carriages poured in
at the gates of the Shaleford ground. An
omnibus full of invited guests arrived from
Shalemouth, and a drag with another large
party from Moreton Basset. Soon the
ground and the Pavilion were quite full;
there had never been so large a meeting at
the Pavilion before.

Miss Priscilla usually went to the dinner,
and stayed through the first quadrille; but
on this occasion she had made up her mind
to remain until the end of the evening.

Barker was a first-rate lady's-maid, but of
late years her services had been so little
required in that line, that she feared she was
growing rusty. On this occasion, however,
she found her work cut out for her, for never
had she remembered Miss Priscilla so difficult to please in the matter of costume and
all the little details of an elaborate toilette.

The old lady was usually content to appear

in a plain black silk, with a bit of old lace here and there; but to-day she had ransacked every drawer and wardrobe in the house, and ferreted out splendours that had not seen the light of day for years.

"Sandshire must be made to understand that I still belong to the house of Trevor," said the old lady to Barker.

Then Barker had understood that Miss Priscilla was going to play the *grande dame*, to the extinction of all Brooms and Hunts, Broughtons and counter folk generally.

Barker entered with zest into the spirit of this new phase in her mistress's life. She did wonders in a few hours, in accommodating fashions of years ago to those of the present day, and she vowed, as Miss Priscilla stood ready to depart in her donkey-carriage, that there would not be a better-dressed lady in the Pavilion.

Miss Priscilla had found in the recesses of

her wardrobe a magnificent brocaded silk, so thick that it would stand up of itself. The ground was of a deep rich bronze colour, and the flowers were marigolds, delicately shaded in browns and golds and greens. Such a silk as is not often seen nowadays, and which had cost a small fortune in the days when the old squire, Miss Priscilla's father, was still alive. Over her shoulders Miss Priscilla had thrown a costly Indian shawl, worth a hundred guineas if it was worth a farthing, and in her brown silk bonnet she had placed white ostrich feathers tipped with glittering gold.

People were quite taken aback by Miss Priscilla's splendour, as she marched sturdily up to that part of the Pavilion where Lady Margate was holding a sort of court as Lady Paramount. Usually she hovered about the verandahs, and had a nod and a smile for every one ; but to-day she was a different

woman. She had sailed up the room as
though she were a queen, her gold-tipped
plumes nodding over her grey hair. She
made a great deal of Diana, and almost
patronised Lady Adela ; then turning to
Lady Margate, she drew that lady aside,
and said :

"You know, my dear, that in general I
prefer to lose myself in the crowd, but to-
night I think of taking the place that is my
right as the oldest member of this club.
Perhaps you will kindly have a place reserved for me at your own table below
yourself and my cousin's wife, but below no
one else."

The "no one else" was so emphatic, that
Lady Margate looked surprised, but she
immediately gave the necessary orders, and
Miss Priscilla's card was placed at the table
where the Lady Paramount would have to
preside.

Planty Broom had been as good as his word. He had taken the tickets himself to "The Willows," had stayed there to luncheon, and had considerably improved the opportunity with Miss Desmoulines. At "The Willows" he had been introduced to Conrad Norton, who had flattered him to the top of his bent; and Planty had gone back to Buncombe bursting with vanity, and full of the praises of the grandson of the celebrated Duc de Vaurien. As soon as Mrs. Astor and her sister appeared at the Pavilion with Conrad Norton, who on this occasion accompanied them, Planty had brought his mother and sister up to them, and had introduced them with his blandest smiles.

Mrs. Broom was affable to a degree. Élise and Genista had made one another's acquaintance at Coddesley. Mrs. Broom suggested that the party should all sit together, and went off to see that those seats were where she wished to be seated. To her surprise and indignation she discovered that her card had been removed from the seat next to the Earl of Margate, and fastened to a chair at a table lower down the room.

"Who has dared move my place?" said Mrs. Broom to an astonished flunkey in the Margate livery.

"It was by her ladyship's orders, ma'am," said the man.

Mrs. Broom said she would soon see whether she would not sit where she pleased, and was untying the card from the chair when a light touch was laid on her stout arm, and Miss Priscilla, in the very blandest but iciest of tones, said:

"Excuse me, Mrs. Broom, but that is my place."

"Excuse me, Miss Trevor, I gave my servant orders to tie my card here, and here I mean to sit."

" I think not, Mrs. Broom," said Miss Priscilla as she quietly slid on to the chair in question, and sat down on it. " As the senior member of the Shaleford Club, my place among the ladies present is next to that of the Lady Paramount. You will find your party have been given their proper position—at the other end."

Mrs. Broom glared in speechless amazement at the little old maid, but she could not actually pull the chair from under her, so, concealing her rage as best she could, she made an undignified retreat to her own party.

There were many tables stretching down the room ; at each table were laid eight places. At the first table, which was placed crosswise at the top of the room, sat the Margates and Captain Norman with the Trevors and Miss Priscilla ; at the next a group of county swells, the Lanes, and

Careys, and Fullers, while Mrs. Broom's party had to content themselves with places far down the room in the neighbourhood of the Hunts and the Broughtons.

Mrs. Broom was furious; but she vowed she would be even with Miss Priscilla yet.

Conversation flagged sadly at the Lady Paramount's table. Lady Margate herself was ill at ease; she knew not what schemes for her own and others' undoing might be in process of hatching in Conrad Norton's fertile brain. Charlie Norman had anticipated an opportunity of meeting Eva on neutral ground; and Diana had looked forward to the "grand day" of the Shaleford Club simply that she might have the society of Victor Ross. Miss Priscilla's heart, as we know, was very sore for the slight that had been put upon those who were most dear to her in all the world; while Lord Margate himself was annoyed that his only other

nominee besides his brother should not have
been elected to the club.

What could not be cured, however, had to
be endured; and Charlie Norman, being seated
next Diana, made himself as agreeable as his
keen disappointment would allow. Perhaps
in his endeavour to mislead his brother as to
the object of his daily visits to the Priory,
Charlie Norman rather overdid his part;
for not only the general public considered
his engagement to Diana a highly probable announcement, but even Mr. Trevor
and Lady Adela, in their conversations
together, dwelt with much calm complacency
upon the turn Diana's affairs seemed to be
taking.

Notwithstanding the rebuff Mrs. Broom
had received, her party was in high feather.
Conrad applied himself with a will to the
capture of outworks, in the persons of Mr.
and Mrs. Broom, before laying siege to the

citadel of Genista's heart and fortune. He
had seen many lands; he was master of
many subjects, and had a superficial knowledge of many more. His conversation was
brilliant, and his flattery both subtle and
artistic.

Genista listened with all her ears to the
tales of adventure, the happy repartees, the
delicately-implied compliments of this descendant of the noble house of Vaurien. She was
too retiring to enter much into the conversation, but she was quite content to look on
and listen, in mute admiration of the beauty
and brilliancy of the man who was keeping
the whole table in good humour with itself
and him.

Planty Broom was in the seventh heaven
of delight with himself, his clothes, and Élise
Desmoulines. At present such was the
order of his affections; but Miss Desmoulines, who was aware of the fact, was

steadily making her way into the second rank, though she hardly expected ever to reach the first.

As to Mrs. Astor, she had quite enough to do to listen to old Broom, whom she drew out at will. She affected sympathy with his past poverty and present magnificence so well, that she found herself entrusted with Mr. Broom's early history; his arrival in the metropolis with the three halfpence; the reluctance with which he parted with the first of the three for two farthing cakes; the horror with which he saw the second disappear into the Thames, as he rashly contemplated the river from the bank; and the manner in which, by patience and perseverance, he had forced the third one to yield a golden harvest to his genius and his will!

Altogether, Mr. Broom's encomiums on the pretty widow, when the dinner was at an end, quite electrified his wife, who, however, paid him back in his own coin by her unlimited praise of Conrad Norton.

When a few toasts had been drunk, the ladies retired to exchange bonnets for flowers, while the men lounged in the verandahs while they smoked.

During this half-hour Lord Margate asked Mrs. Astor to introduce him and his brother to Conrad Norton. He was startled not a little at the strong resemblance between the two young men; but, as Élise had once said, the likeness wore off on further acquaintance.

In Norman's face there was perhaps more real power, but less brilliancy. He was stouter built than Norton — smarter even, in a military sense, but not so graceful, nor, as Americans would say, so elegant. The chief difference, however, lay in the expression. There was equal boldness in the eyes of both, but in Norton's face there was a shifting, pained unrest. His eyes were never still.

CHAPTER XVII.

THE DANCE AT THE PAVILION.

HE band struck up the first qua
drille. Every one was supposed to
join in this ; it was a sort of Shaleford ceremonial. The secretary of the club
danced with the Lady Paramount; Lord Margate led out Lady Adela Trevor ; Mr.
Broughton, as treasurer, danced with the
secretary's wife, to that lady's deep mortifi-
cation and disgust. Even Miss Priscilla
picked up her brocaded train, and made her

steps with the best of them, with her cousin, Mr. Trevor, for a partner.

When Cupid is absent, Terpsichore is supreme. Provided that the woman a man loves is out of the way, the woman whose waltzing is the poetry of motion commands that man so long as the dance continues. So it was with Captain Norman. He was a perfect waltzer, and he loved waltzing as one of the fine arts. Diana matched him. She was the right height; she danced the same step; she was a musician, as well as a *danseuse*. She knew, as he did, that waltzing is not a mere physical recreation; in its perfection, it is a subtle expression of the brain's fancy, intellectual, sensuous, and silent.

One turn with Captain Norman decided Diana that, if he asked her, she would gladly give him every "round" on her card. He did ask her for all the waltzes; and as Captain Norman was Captain Norman, Lady

Adela did not interfere. The galops they kept for semi-duty dances; the polkas and "squares" they sat out.

Was it wonderful that Sandshire said they were engaged?

Planty Broom did not shine in the *trois-temps*, as Miss Desmoulines very soon found to her cost. A twirl with a galvanised clothes-horse would have been an improvement upon Planty as a partner. He carried one leg round with him, while he slid about upon the other, as though he were executing figures upon ice. He used his left arm like the tube of a trombone, and let fly at moments that were inopportune for his neighbours. If his gyrations were not as frenziedly comic as those of Mr. Pericles Bone, who danced much as if he had been a nervous prawn set up on its tail, still they were of a class that could only have done credit to a two-pronged fork, or a dance on a pair of stilts.

Miss Desmoulines, however, expressed her-self as enraptured.

" It is so seldom I find any one who can dance my step," she said, as she succeeded in landing herself breathless and bruised on a bench.

" I think we get on pretty well," he replied with affected modesty.

" It was. divine !" she exclaimed. " You dance so lightly and in such perfect time. You learnt abroad, doubtless—so few Eng-lishmen can dance."

" No, I have never learnt. I have a good ear, and I picked it up as best I could."

" Really ! Well, I am sure your proficiency does you infinite credit. That waltz was quite heavenly !"

" Would it be asking too much to request the honour of another ?"

" I could dance with you all night with

pleasure, only of course you are in such great request."

"I don't see that a man need make a martyr of himself to social considerations. Girls about here can't dance my step."

"If they only knew what they lost, they would be careful to learn."

"I shall throw over my other partners if you will honour me, Miss Desmoulines."

"Oh! indeed no! I could not be so selfish. There are other girls who must have come on purpose to get a dance with you. It would not be fair to them."

"Well, perhaps not; but you will give me all the galops and a couple of polkas, will you not?"

"With pleasure; you may write down what you please."

"But I see you are engaged for most of the 'rounds,'" said he, as he took the offered card, " at least there are initials against most of them."

" Men bothered me for dances before dinner. Had I known you would have cared to ask me, I would have kept my card free ; as it is, I shall throw the men over ; as you say, one cannot martyr one's self for social considerations."

Planty, intoxicated with flattery, scrawled his name over Miss Desmoulines' card, on which she had purposely inscribed fictitious initials from end to end.

Then Conrad claimed her for a dance, and she told him of her little manœuvre.

" Come up and claim his dances, you know, and make as much fuss as you can," she said to Conrad. " When he gets cross, say something handsome, and give me up. The booby would swallow a whale if one had no more delicate bait."

" I think of going to stay at Buncombe,"

said Conrad. "I have not been invited yet, but I have been playing up to it with the old woman. I have given Anne a hint, and I think you might be even more explicit with that young whipper-snapper. If I once get a berth there, I can manage for all of us so much better than I can at the 'Trevor Arms.'"

"A very good idea; but if you do, you will have to pay your hotel bill."

"Not at all; that is a thing I make a point of never doing, at any rate with my own money. It has become quite a matter of principle with me of late years, I assure you."

"I have no doubt you are quite able to take care of yourself, Con. Tell me, why do you so avoid the Margates?"

"I have not avoided them, but my acquaintance with Lady Margate is but slight. When I knew her she had not become a countess. If they wish to encourage the acquaintance, they are at liberty to do so."

" What line do you mean to take with Genista ?'

" Oh ! the Othello and Desdemona line is evidently the best. Did you see how she sat with her mouth wide open, when I displayed so much inventive fancy at dinner ? She wants a hero. That curate fellow is not heroic, neither am I ; but I have a good memory and a ready imagination."

" Then all those tales of adventure you told at dinner were inventions ?"

" Pure and simple as far as I am concerned. I got the facts from a Spanish romance, and as I know Spain fairly well, I put myself in the hero's place."

" Con, you are an ornament to the profession !"

He laughed—a bright, low, musical laugh. There was nothing of the Mephistopheles about this man ; no slow music accompanied him, nor lurid flame. How beautiful he was, with his white skin and lustrous eyes, and his strong lithe figure and bright smile.

"Here is Planty Broom coming back for you," he said. "Now I am off to work the oracle with Mrs. Broom."

"I thought you had forgotten me," said Élise to Planty, as Conrad moved away.

"As if that were possible," said he, looking boldly into her eyes.

"This young man has been refreshing himself," said Élise to herself. "All the better; I only hope he is given that way." Then aloud: "You should have come up a moment sooner, Mr. Broom; some one has been paying you a compliment."

"Really," said Planty, pricking up his ears. "I hope you endorsed it."

"That is as may be; at any rate I had not time to do so in words."

"I am dying to hear what it was."

" Do not raise your expectations too high ; it was not a lady who paid it you."

" Not a lady ! Oh, then I am not curious at all."

" Coming from a man, it is at any rate sure to be genuine."

" That is very prettily put."

" Mr. Norton admires your dancing so much ; he said it was like a poem."

" What bosh !"

" But not so much as your seat on horseback. He says it is quite a sight to see you on your bay mare."

" I did not know that he had seen me."

" Poor Mr. Norton ! I am afraid he is fearfully bored at that little inn. He came away from all his gaieties in town simply to be of service to us, as we were ' unprotected females.' We supposed ' The Willows ' would have been large enough for us to have offered him a room for a week or two, but

we find it is scarcely large enough for ourselves."

" I wonder how he amuses himself; he has
no horses with him, has he ?"

" No, he has left them behind. It hardly
seemed worth while, you know, to bring them
over."

" Bring them over ! What do you mean ?
Does Mr. Norton live in Ireland ?"

Elise laughed a little amused laugh.

" No, no !" she said, " at his own place in
France. His home is in France, you
know."

" No, I did not know. Where does he
live ? in Paris ?"

" The Vaurien estates are in the depart-
ment of the Sarthe."

" Oh ! he has estates in France, has he ?"

" Not yet, but he spends a good deal of
time there ; his mother, you know, was a
daughter of the old Duc de Vaurien ; quite

of the *crême de la crême* of the *ancien régime*."

"So you told me at Coddesley. What is the name of the Duc's place ?"

"Château Blague," said Élise, without a moment's hesitation, "not far from Blague-ville sur Sarthe."

"Where is Sarthe ? Is it a mountain or a city ?"

"The Sarthe is a river. It falls into the Loire at Angers. *You* ought to be up in the geography of that district, Mr. Broom. Both streams are in the part of *la belle* France which was once Anjou."

"Oh, really !" said Planty, who did not know where "Anjou" was any more than the home of the Choktaw Indians. "Shall we take another turn ?"

"Will you mind my telling you something, Mr. Broom, something that you are not quite perfect in ?" said Élise, after another fearful plunge into the mazy dance, in which she was knocked completely out of time by Planty's bad steering.

"I could bear to hear anything from your lips except one."

"And what is that?"

Then he gazed into her dark eyes again, saying, "Except that you did not—like me."

He had almost said "love me," but refrained in time—"like me" might mean anything.

"I shall never say that, Mr. Broom," said Élise softly, lowering her lashes. "You have been so kind, so very kind to me. May I tell you what you are not perfect in?"

"I am all attention."

"Perhaps I ought not to say it; but, if I am mock-modest, our steps will not go so perfectly together as otherwise they would; so I will tell you. You hold me so far from you; you leave me too much to my own helplessness!"

"Is that all?" said Planty, as they tore away again into the throng. "It is a fault that is soon remedied." And, suiting the action to the word, he pressed her closer, closer still, till each could feel the other's heart-beats as they rushed along.

Though the strains of Strauss did not move him to unwonted energy, her beauty, more sensuous than music, was beginning to weave its spell around him, and to steep his senses in intoxicating delight.

When the dance was over, he led her silently out into the verandah, and then farther afield into the shadows of the archery ground. A path led down from the grass to the bank of the Shale, and on the bank was a rustic bench, hidden from the pavilion by a sycamore-tree. To this he led her.

She almost felt that she had gone too far.

She had stirred his passions ; she had set his brain on fire ; but the chain with which she had fettered him was but one of flame.　To-morrow it would cool, and the man would repent.　She must not listen to him now. If she gave him rope enough, he would hang himself, safe enough ; but she must have him declare himself openly, before witnesses.

His arm was round her, his breath came hot upon her cheek.

He longed to kiss her, but as yet he did not dare.

" How beautiful you are," he said.

She toyed with her fan, but she did not reply.　Would he be fool enough to ask her to be his wife ?　Élise was keen, but she did not know Mr. Planty Broom as yet.　He was weak, and easily moved by a woman's beauty ; but he was not such a fool as he looked.

A tress of her hair was blown loose by the

breeze, and floated across his cheek. He kissed it before he returned it to its sister locks.

The silence became embarrassing. " You are cold," at last he said. " Come closer."

She nestled a little nearer. Her head was almost on his shoulder. He bent down and kissed her on the lips.

Shadows crossed their vision. Standing so close that they must have seen it all, were Conrad and Genista.

Élise started back. She did not know if Genista had seen who she was in the dim shadow. Other footsteps approached. She stood up and took Planty's arm.

" We had better go back," she said.

Both were annoyed at the interruption. She had wanted an offer of marriage, and he had wanted, what ?—more kisses.

CHAPTER XVIII.

WHILE Norman was giving society grounds for supposing that he wished to make Diana Trevor the future Countess of Margate, while Miss Desmoulines was angling for the "Broomsprig," and Conrad was influencing Genista's heart by invented tales of his personal adventures, Miss Priscilla was developing a spirit of intrigue that would have done credit to the court of Catherine de Médicis.

For more years than most people cared to
remember, Miss Priscilla had been a homely
person, with homely tastes ; kind of heart,
without ambition, pursuing the even tenor of
her peaceful life in charity with all the neighbourhood.   She was known to be well off,
and to have put by money for many years ;
while she spent but little, and that little even
upon the poor of Olton Priors, and on hospitality, never upon herself.

The non-election of Victor Ross may seem
a small thing to have caused a complete
change in Miss Priscilla ; but, nevertheless,
there was a change, and this had been the
cause.

So long as Eva had been too young to
enter society, Miss Priscilla had contented
herself with seeing her god-daughter almost
daily, and fulfilling a mother's part to the
best of her ability ; but Eva was now
eighteen.   She had appeared in public, as a

grown-up woman, at Miss Priscilla's garden-party, for the first time; and the old lady had thought it best to let things take their natural course with regard to her introduction into county circles.

When Miss Priscilla had seconded Lord Margate, as proposer of Victor's name, for the Shaleford Club, she had supposed it impossible that the combined claims of the houses of Norman and Trevor would have been disregarded and set aside. Yet so it had been. Victor Ross had been the only candidate who had failed to obtain admittance. It was an insult to Victor, to his family, to Lord Margate, and to Miss Priscilla! It had, moreover, touched the old lady in her tenderest points:—her intense devotion to the Ross family, and her own pride of birth. These must both be vindicated. The Rosses should be sought after far and near; and Olton Priors should understand that the power of the house of Trevor, in that part of the world, had by no means diminished.

"My dear," said Miss Priscilla to Lady Margate, as they stood together in the Pavilion, "I am sure you would do an old lady a favour, when such is in your power, and I have one to ask of you."

"Assuredly, Miss Priscilla. If there is anything I can do, you know how gladly it will be done."

"My god-daughter, Eva Ross, comes out this year. She was allowed to 'peep out' at my little gathering the other afternoon ; but the party was not of sufficient importance for it to be considered my god-daughter's *début*. Her mother was my oldest and dearest friend. She was a Leslie, you know, and very highly connected ; and though the man she married was not quite in her own rank, he was one of nature's noblemen. I feel responsible for the launching of her children into their mother's sphere. I cannot give a ball at the Manor House ; it is too small. Lady Adela is a new comer, though, as my Eva is much at the Priory, she would, perhaps, be the proper person to introduce Miss Ross to Sandshire. We are just in the midst of our summer gaieties, and I wish my god-daughter to join in them. I should take it as a personal favour to myself if you would call on her."

"Most certainly I will. I had intended doing so, and had told Mr. Ross my intention ; but I will put it off no longer now. You may rely on my driving over to Black Rock to-morrow."

"Thank you very much ; and while so many of our set are assembled here, do you not think it would be a good opportunity to ask others to do the same ? I will speak to several ; and may I hope you will do so also ?"

"Certainly. I am now going to dance with Colonel Lane; I will manage all you wish." And Lady Margate nodded gaily to Miss Priscilla, and took her place for a quadrille.

The old lady wandered from group to group, and made the same request. Only to the best old families did she appeal, the Fullers and Careys and Lanes; if they once called, the Pryce-Tynkers and others would be sure to follow.

Presently Miss Priscilla espied Camilla Howard sitting alone. The girl looked dispirited and ill at case. She did not know the "county" set; she wished to avoid the "counter." Between the two she had come to the ground. Camilla loved dancing; but, on this her first entrance into higher circles, she felt neglected and forlorn and dull.

"That girl spoke up for my boy," said the

old lady to herself. Then she got up and crossed the room to where Camilla sat all alone.

"Not dancing!" she said, in her kindest manner; "what can the young men be thinking of?"

"We are almost strangers here," answered Camilla, brightening up at such pointed notice from Miss Priscilla.

"But you know Mr. Broom and Mr. Bone, and there are others too."

"Mr. Broom has not asked me."

"You have a long life in which to be thankful for being spared such an infliction," ejaculated the old lady.

"And I cannot dance Mr. Bone's step. It is so very—very peculiar. I tried once, but I dare not do it again."

"I do not think you are the loser; but you dance beautifully, Miss Howard, and I do not wish my young gentlemen friends to lose a chance of enjoyment ; may I introduce some of them to you ?"

Camilla beamed with delight as she assented.

" Have you a dance to spare, Captain Norman ?" said Miss Priscilla, going up to the young man, as he was standing by Diana.

" For Miss Priscilla certainly, yes," said he, with a smile.

" My dancing days are over, but I am still vain enough to believe that young men will do me a favour, and dance with me by proxy."

Norman bowed laughingly. " Who is the lady ?" said he.

" The next best dancer in the room, next to Diana—Camilla Howard."

" Pray introduce me ; Miss Trevor, will you excuse me ?"

" A 'round' you know ; I never accepted a 'square' with a perfect waltzer when I was a girl; and I expect the same honours paid to my proxy."

"A 'round' it shall be, Miss Priscilla. Can you spare me the next galop?" he added, to Camilla, when the introduction had been made.

Camilla was delighted. She had so longed for one dance with the best dancer in the room, but she had deemed it an impossibility.

Then Miss Priscilla led up Colonel Lane, a grey-haired, aristocratic-looking man, who had been in the Guards, and one of the young Careys, and a dancing parson from Shalemouth, and soon Camilla's empty card was full.

While Camilla was waiting for one of her partners, the old lady said:

"I mean to ask a very few young people to meet my god-daughter, Miss Ross, at dinner next week. Do you think Mrs. Howard would trust you and your sister under my chaperonage?"

" I am sure she would," said Camilla.

" Then, suppose we say Monday, at seven
o'clock. Quite a quiet dinner, you know;
my rooms are small; I have not had an opportunity of being civil to Mrs. Astor yet; I
shall ask her and her sister, and Mr. Norton;
and Victor Ross's friend, Mr. George Warre."

Then the old lady turned away to speak to
Lord Margate, so that she did not see the
crimson flush that mounted to Camilla's cheek
at this last announcement.

Miss Priscilla passed over to where Mrs.
Astor was sitting next to Mrs. Broom. Mrs.
Broom scowled. Miss Priscilla did not take
any notice whatever of Mrs. Broom.

" I have asked a few great friends to dinner
on Monday night, Mrs. Astor," said Miss
Priscilla, with an emphasis on "great;" "may
I hope for the pleasure of seeing you and
Miss Desmoulines?"

" We shall be delighted, Miss Priscilla."

" If you will bring Mr. Norton, I shall be very glad to see him ; I will write him a note, of course ; but he will understand that I have no gentleman relation to send to pay him a formal visit."

" Oh yes ! he will quite understand. I feel sure that he will be delighted to avail himself of your invitation."

Then Miss Priscilla sent for her " Jehu;" and Beer appeared with the well-known donkeys and carriage. Miss Priscilla was very over-done, and, when she arrived at home, she hurried to her room, and had a good cry all by herself. It did not last long, however, for the faithful Barker, saying " that was just what she had expected," appeared with a strong cup of tea, the tortoise-shell Tom, and much friendly consolation.

CHAPTER XIX.

WHEN the Brooms got home to Buncombe after the dance at the Pavilion, there was much to be said before any one retired to rest.

"I think Miss Priscilla's conduct is atrocious," burst out Mrs. Broom, as she sipped the soup that was always provided on their return from such festivities. "Who is she, indeed, that she should give herself such airs?"

" I told you it would be so, Belinda," said her husband, " when you were so determined to blackball young Ross ; Miss Priscilla doats on that young man. You have made a false move, my dear, and I don't see how you are going to recover it."

" I am sure I wouldn't trouble my head about that old cat," said Planty, who, having had a good deal more wine than was good for him, was cooling himself with a brandy and soda ; " and as to that hulking brute Ross, his admission would be a disgrace to the club ; a fellow who works all day in his shirt-sleeves, stacking timber on the wharf, to come and mix with us in the ballroom ! it's absurd !"

" But he dined at Coddesley, Planty," said Genista meekly. " If Lord Margate chooses to receive him, I do not see that our snubbing him will do any good to us or harm to him."

"Nobody ever supposed you could see anything," said her amiable brother. "Ross is a low lout of a carpenter, that's what he is. Fancy a man claiming to be a gentleman wrestling with all the common navvies at the Moreton Basset Fair!"

"Ah! he won the first prize, did he not?" said Mr. Broom.

"Yes, but he gave the money to the Wrestlers' Fund!" exclaimed Genista.

"How do you know so much about it?" sneered Planty.

"Camilla Howard told me. She heard it from young George Warre."

"The innkeeper's son! Ross's bosom friend! You can tell what sort of a man Ross is, by his knowing only one man intimately in the place, and that man a coarse prizefighting brute like Warre."

"Mr. Norton seems to find the society of the 'prizefighting brute,' as you call him, agreeable enough ; he is always about with him."

" Because he is a stranger in a strange land, and has no one else to make a companion of. Miss Desmoulines told me to-night he was bored to death at the Trevor Arms. Why not ask him here, governor? he seems no end of a good fellow."

" I have no objection, my dear boy, if your mother has not."

" He is very agreeable—very," said Mrs. Broom ; " but we know nothing of him— absolutely nothing ;" and as she caught her husband's eye she glanced meaningly at Genista.

" Oh ! I have heard all about him," said Planty. " His mother was a daughter of the Duc de Vaurien of Château Blague, Blagueville-sur-Sarthe, not far from Angers ; and he spends much of his time there, and lives quite among the *crême de la crême* of the *ancien régime*."

"Bless the boy!" exclaimed Mr. Broom, "whence this sudden blossoming into unknown tongues?"

"Miss Desmoulines told me all about him, governor; she has known him ever since she was quite a child, and she can't say enough good of him."

"Mrs. Astor seems an excellent person," said Mr. Broom, "and if her sister is like her, they must be very well conducted young women."

Planty thought of the kiss under the sycamore tree, and glanced at his sister to see if she had seen that little innocent amusement; but Genista was making her napkin-ring do duty for a boomerang; and was too intent upon compelling its return to the spot from whence it started, to take any notice of the remark.

"She seems a very commonplace little widow, Mr. Broom," said his wife, who thought her husband's attentions had been far too marked for good taste.

"Little, and a widow, but certainly not common-place," answered her husband. "What do you think she has been employed about ever since her husband's death ?"

"Flirting with married men, I dare say," said his wife ; "she seems to follow up that line with considerable success."

"My dear Belinda, how can you be so absurd ! She is a most harmless little creature. She has been starting working-men's clubs in London ; and has organised a reading-room for the railway porters at Victoria. She told me so herself, and her heart seems to be thoroughly in the work."

"And she is going to take a district in Olton Priors, mamma," said Genista. "She was asking me all about the poor people, this evening, and she has chosen the worst district of all, down by Low Wick. She says helping those who are in suffering like herself, is the only balm for a widowed heart."

" Only fiddlestick !" said Mrs. Broom sharply. " She will take some other balm the first chance she has of getting it, I'll be bound. However, as your father seems so very anxious to improve the acquaintance of these people, of course I have nothing more to say." .

" My dear, no one has suggested Mrs. Astor being asked to stay here. It was Planty, not I, who wished Mr. Norton to be invited."

" It is all the same thing," said Mrs. Broom. " Of course if the man hangs up his hat in our hall, we shall have the others in and out at all times of the day ; and probably Mrs. Astor, while procuring ' balm for her widowed heart,' will get all sorts of infectious diseases and bring them up here to us."

"Joking apart, Belinda, if Planty wants Mr. Norton asked here, I see no objection to it. Mrs. Astor has her own house, and her own occupations."

"Procuring balm for her widowed heart," snapped Mrs. Broom.

"And is not likely to take the trouble to walk two miles to Buncombe in such broiling weather as we are having now."

"It is so confoundedly slow, mother," said Planty, "always having to ride alone; and since Norman has got spooney on that little spitfire at the Priory, I am duller than ever."

"Well, my dear boy, I give way. Heaven knows I would do anything on earth to make you happy and contented at home. And now do you and Genista go to bed; for I want to talk to your father."

Though Mrs. Broom spoilt her son and

paid but small attention to her daughter, she exercised an extraordinary influence over both. She possessed tact and a firm will; but in her anxiety to see Planty freed from temptations by marriage, she forgot that she might only be helping him out of the frying-pan into the fire.

"William," said she, as soon as her children had left the room, "I do not think you see how serious matters are becoming. I had hoped at one time that Planty would have taken a fancy to Miss Trevor, but he has not, and I am sure he will not; besides, the girl is as good as engaged to Captain Norman. On the other hand, our boy has fallen head over ears in love with Miss Desmoulines. Is it to be allowed to go on, or is it not?"

"My dear, what can we do one way or the other? Planty is five-and-twenty, and has a will of his own."

"That has nothing to do with it. Planty's will can be crushed quite as easily as other people's. If we do not give him the money, he cannot marry any one."

"Are you sure that he wants to *marry* Miss Desmoulines?"

"William!"

"My dear, let us call a spade a spade; Planty is passionately in love with this young lady—I admit that—I can see it for myself. Besides, he is at 'The Willows' now every day, and all day long; but you must remember that this is not the first time in our experience that Planty has been similarly afflicted."

"But, William, you cannot suppose for a moment that this affair could terminate as others, alas! have terminated. Miss Desmoulines is a lady of birth and position, the descendant of an old French family, and the daughter of a German baroness. We have had enough to pay already to hush up Planty's escapades, but this affair is surely one of quite another sort."

"You mistook my meaning, Belinda; of course to a lady like Miss Desmoulines, Planty can propose nothing but marriage; nor had I any other idea in my mind when I spoke; but Planty, in his way, is very keen; I do not think he is so desperately smitten as to offer to share all his worldly goods with this superb young woman. If it is only a strong flirtation, but strong enough to compromise Miss Desmoulines — what then?"

Mrs. Broom shrugged her shoulders. "A lady of Miss Desmoulines' position could hardly claim damages if you mean that," she said.

"That is just what I do mean. Planty is so—so ardent, that he is struck with a fresh face every day; if he goes on playing the fool with this girl, he will burn his fingers, for he will not be able to hush the matter up as has been done with obscure farmers' daughters and barmaids before now to our cost."

"No! indeed!" said Mrs. Broom with a sigh. "That is just the reason why I am so anxious to get him settled, William; if the scandals of the last year or two are suffered to go on, it will break my heart."

"I see no objection to his marrying Miss Desmoulines."

"Nor I, if she loves him; but does she love him? that is the question. She knows he is rich. It may be only his money that she is after; but to go to another subject, have you noticed how attracted Genista is by Mr. Conrad Norton?"

"Pshaw! my dear, the man was only introduced to her to-day."

"What has that to do with it? Love at

first sight is most dangerous, because least founded on reason."

" Genista has too much sense."

Mrs. Broom shook her head. " Believe me, my dear, sense is not to be expected in these cases. Genista, moreover, is romantic and impulsive; her head is crammed with heroes and heroines, and she is so plain herself, that beauty plays an absurdly disproportionate part on her life's stage. If Captain Norman had paid her any attention, she would have loved him to distraction, and our highest dreams of ambition would have been realised at the same time. But it is no use sighing after the moon. Captain Norman does not care a rap for Genista, and never will; he is entirely taken up with that wretched. little Trevor girl, who I wish was at the bottom of the sea, with every other Trevor in the county. However, that has nothing to do with the present subject. As

I was saying, **Genista** might have cared for Lord Margate's brother, if he had cared for her; and I am quite sure that she did care for him, just enough to make her **take an** additionally strong interest in a man so like the Captain as is Mr. Norton."

" How about the curate, Belinda? **You** said only the other day that you thought we ought to make inquiries about Mr. Channing's family and prospects, because he was paying Genista so much attention."

" My dear, you are a practical man, with **no** nerves, **no** sentiment, and no imagination."

" Thank you kindly for your good opinion," said Mr. Broom mockingly.

" You have been a dear good husband to me, William, and you have a wife who knows what a good husband means ; but you imagine that every other human being must necessarily think and act in the same groove as yourself,

and you never make allowances for differ-
ences of training and disposition. Planty,
in character, takes after me. If he were
more like you, my dear, it would have been
the better for himself and us ; but goodness
knows where Genista came from. She is all
nerves and fancies, and longings after the
beautiful. In a word, she is what is now
called ' æsthetic.' Foiled in worshipping the
beautiful in a lover, she has turned to it in
art and religion. You don't know the difference between the ' Old Hundredth ' and
' Pop goes the Weasel ;' and if they were
both played slow to me on the organ, in my
best bonnet in the family pew, I don't
think I should be any wiser than you. But
Genista is a musician and has a true artist's
love of both form and colour. " Mr. Channing is an artist. He and Genista sympa-
thise. Mr. Channing is a musician. He
and Genista harmonise. Mr. Channing

is a deeply religious man ; being æsthetic, his religion takes an æsthetic form ; every colour is a symbol, every form is a type of something in the spiritual world. Naturally enough his influence has so wrought upon Genista, that she has ceased to be able to separate her love of the work from her love of the worker. To us copes and berrettas, lights and flower-pots, vestments and altar-cloths may be summed up in Planty's favourite slang word 'bosh,' but to a mind like Genista's, in which legitimate emotion is repressed, the craving after such things is natural. I have said so much because I want you to see to what end all this tends. If you ask Mr. Norton to the house, he will supply Genista with an outlet for all her devotion. He is fascinating, accomplished, and beautiful as a god. Ritualism will go to the wall. The curate's influence will die out. Have I made myself fully

understood ?" Mrs. Broom here paused for
lack of breath, and awaited her husband's
answer.

"Most fully. You are a clever woman,
my dear, and if I do not ask Mr. Norton
here——"

"Genista will marry the curate, care for
him in a mild, vague, feeble sort of way, talk
about his goodness, his kindness, and his
devotion to the church. If she has children,
she will transfer her love to them, and keep
a dutiful regard for their father as their
father; which will require to be warmed up
afresh at intervals, by religious fervour and
domestic sorrows."

"What a horrible picture ! One can see
where Genista's imagination comes from, at
my rate. Am I to gather from it that you
do not wish Genista to marry Mr. Channing ?"

"I had hitherto regarded such a marriage

as the only alternative to her being an old maid."

" I do not see anything to lead us to suppose that Mr. Norton has found Genista attractive."

" Mrs. Astor tells me that he is very much struck with her."

" There is not much to go upon in that."

" I feel we ought to give her a chance of marrying where she can really love, even though there is the danger of her affection not being returned."

" But what do we know of this young Adonis ?"

" We must find out."

" How ?"

" England is small. English society is smaller. The man has the bearing of a gentleman. We should be certain to find out anything there might be against him, I should think."

" But Vaurien is a French title. Château Blague is a French country seat. The man says his father died when he was a child, and that he has no relations in England."

" Lady Margate is distantly connected with him."

" Ah ! true, I had forgotten that ; but no one knows who she was before her marriage."

" I do not think we need trouble ourselves to insist on good birth in a son-in-law, and Genista will have enough money for both. If this Mr. Norton is a gentleman, and bears a respectable character, I confess I should like to see Genista settled. She is not attractive. She is not in the first flush of youth. We cannot hope that she will make a brilliant match, and I am averse to her marrying the curate."

" Then you wish me to ask Mr. Norton ?"

" I think we must risk it. If he is vicious, or a fortune-hunter, or a mushroom, I shall be able to detect him better under my own roof."

"You understand these things better than I do, my dear; let it be as you wish."

"I will see Lady Margate myself to-morrow; but I cannot ask her pointed questions without seeming to be inquisitive about her own past life."

"Do so; and now let us be off to bed, I am tired to death."

CHAPTER XX.

THE next day Mrs. Broom did call on Lady Margate, as she had stated her intention of doing, but Lady Margate was out.

Being in the Olton Priors direction, Mrs. Broom went on to " The Willows." The ladies were at home. Mrs. Broom thought she might glean some fresh knowledge of Conrad Norton's career; but she approached the subject warily.

After discussing several topics of local

interest, she led the conversation round to foreign travel, to French society, and so to the Duc de Vaurien and Château Blague.

"You have stayed with Madame Norton, I presume," said Mrs. Broom to Mrs. Astor, "as you are such an old friend of Mr. Norton's family?"

"No, indeed," answered Mrs. Astor, who had noted every change in the conversation, and knew perfectly well what Mrs. Broom had come for. "Our connection with his family was chiefly on his father's side. My father, Mr. Desmoulines, remembered meeting the old Duc de Vaurien in Paris, when my father was in the service of the government of that day; and he used to tell us stories of the old gentleman's excessive pride of birth. But Madame Norton was dead before we were acquainted with the family, and we have never been in France, though we are ourselves, of course, French by extraction."

"Mr. Norton's father," said Élise, who felt that her sister's account might be embellished without detriment, "was at one time in the Guards, I believe. He met Mademoiselle de Vaurien in Paris, and a love affair on both sides soon ended in a marriage."

"Who is the present possessor of the title ?" asked Mrs. Broom.

" It has become merged in some other family name, I really do not at the moment remember what," said Élise, equal to the occasion. "There was no son, and the nearest male heir was some cousin or other, a Marquis de Bréda or some such name as that. The last Duc de Vaurien had several daughters, one of whom still lives at Château Blague. She is a widow, and I do not know her name, but I believe Mr. Norton inherits largely on her death."

All this seemed circumstantial enough, and it was glibly spoken ; but of course Mrs. Broom was entirely ignorant of French law and French customs.

Mrs. Broom pondered much over what she heard. If Mrs. Astor and Miss Desmoulines were to be trusted, Mr. Norton would be a very desirable son-in-law, far more desirable than the curate. Mrs. Broom hesitated, talked over the matter once more with her husband, called again on Lady Margate, but only to hear that Lord Margate had become suddenly so much worse that he and Lady Margate had both gone to London to procure the best advice. Then Mrs. Broom determined to act on her own responsibility. She sat down and wrote a guarded note to Mr. Norton, in which she said that she had heard he intended staying a week longer in the neighbourhood, and that she hoped he would no longer put up at an hotel, but spend the week with them at Buncombe.

" If we don't like the man, we shall get rid of him at the end of a week, at any rate," said Mrs. Broom, as she sent down the invitation to the Trevor Arms.

Little did Mrs. Broom know Mr. Conrad Norton.

Lady Margate had called upon Eva Ross the very day after the dance at the Pavilion. Lord Margate had accompanied her, but Captain Norman had excused himself. While Lady Margate was at Black Rock, the Lanes and the Fullers both called, so it was soon bruited abroad in the neighbourhood that the Rosses had been taken up by all the best people.

On returning to Coddesley, Lord Margate had been taken very ill. He fainted continually, and brought up blood, which caused his wife great alarm. So terrified was she, that she persuaded Lord Margate to go to London, in order that doctors might have a consultation on his case. On the Saturday, therefore, as he was a little better, they started, intending to return the following week. They took a valet and lady's-maid with them, and left Charlie Norman in charge of Coddesley.

When Miss Priscilla heard of this, she asked Captain Norman to join her dinner-party on the Monday, an invitation he gladly accepted, for he felt pretty sure that at the Manor House he would meet the woman who had now become all the world to him.

Miss Priscilla felt that Lady Adela would probably object to Diana's meeting a man in George Warre's position, and had, partly on that account, and partly on others, purposely avoided asking her on that occasion.

Prompted by Barker, Miss Priscilla had, at the last moment, asked Pericles Bone. Barker, who always knew all the gossip of the town, had said that " the young sawbones was after one of ' them ' Howards," and as Miss Priscilla wanted a twelfth to make out her number, Pericles Bone was invited.

Miss Priscilla was in her cheeriest mood. She loved to see Tom Ross at the bottom of her table. He always sat there when he dined with Miss Priscilla. When Élise Desmoulines found that Diana Trevor was not to be of the party, she decided on making hay while the sun shone ; and she devoted her whole energies to making a friend of Victor Ross.

Élise was handsome, clever, and unscrupulous. She knew perfectly well that if she made love to Victor while he was worshipping at another shrine, he would first suspect her, and then avoid her. In her heart of hearts she detested Diana, and she certainly meant to detach Victor from her, if she could ; but her present object was to form a close friendship with Victor, and evidently Diana Trevor was the best medium for such a scheme.

Almost every one else in the place believed that Captain Norman was in love with Diana, and were in daily expectation of the announcement of the engagement; but Élise and Mrs. Astor knew better.

It so happened that Élise went in to dinner with Victor Ross, and this gave her the opportunity she had so long desired. Mrs. Astor, from the opposite side of the table, watched her sister keenly, as did Captain Norman; but if they expected to see her make love to Victor, they were disappointed. Élise kept different bait for different fish. She knew the difference between Victor Ross and Planty Broom.

She soon managed to turn the conversation

to the Trevor family, without directly mentioning Diana.

"Lady Adela seems to me a type of all that is aristocratic," said she; "she is such a perfect gentlewoman, and her repose of manner is quite delightful."

"She is unlike most Englishwomen, to my mind," said Victor. "I suppose fifteen years spent on the Continent does change people's manners. I sometimes think Lady Adela is too polished."

"I know what you mean; but I should have said Mr. Trevor was even more like burnished steel. He is so courteous, so punctilious, and so fastidious, that I always feel quite afraid of him."

"I think very highly of them both," said Victor, in a tone that implied something about them that he thought capable of improvement; "but I confess I find them difficult to get on with. Lady Adela is cold and uncertain, and Mr. Trevor, though he is always the same whenever one meets him, has a certain reserve and hauteur, which seem to warn people away from any attempts at familiarity, or even intimacy."

"But I am sure Miss Trevor is quite the reverse of that," said Élise. "Her brightness and frank cordiality act like sunbeams on every one with whom she comes in contact. It does me good to sit and watch her, with her sparkling eyes and gay smile. She is very, very charming, to my mind."

Victor was a simple-minded man, so truthful and honest, that he believed the rest of the world to be truthful and honest too. He supposed Élise to be truthful, and his heart warmed towards a woman who spoke so cordially in approval of the girl who was the idol of his being.

His handsome face flushed with pleasure;

but he was by nature reserved, and he felt that he had no right as yet to be enthusiastic on the subject of Diana. Still it was very pleasant to talk, all through dinner, to a handsome woman who evinced utter sympathy with him in the one subject that occupied all his thoughts, namely, Diana Trevor and her various perfections. Victor's interest in Miss Desmoulines increased greatly. She said such very handsome things of Miss Trevor, of Lady Adela, of Miss Trevor's father, and, most of all, of Miss Priscilla.

"We have heard so much of your ' Wilderness ' at Black Rock," she said. "We hear everything is allowed to grow at will. How beautiful it must be."

"It is very beautiful," he replied. " I hope you and Mrs. Astor will come and see it; my sister is very proud of it."

"May I bring Mr. Norton as well ? He is so anxious to know you more intimately,

Mr. Ross. Mr. Warre is enthusiastic about his friends, you know, and he has imbued Mr. Norton with his opinions of you."

Again simple-hearted Victor flushed with pleasure. Being appreciated by one's friends is only second to being loved by the darling of one's heart. He flushed so ingenuously, that Élise began to think she might have gone too far. If the man guessed that she was making love to him, he would fight shy of her at once, and all her hopes would vanish into thin air; so she hastened to prove to him how sincerely friendly she meant to be, but nothing more.

" I fear Lord Margate must be very ill," she said presently, " or they would not have gone off so suddenly to London for advice."

" He has been in wretched health for two years past; I fancy every one but Lady Margate was prepared for his becoming suddenly worse."

"How unlike the brothers are; Captain Norman is so very handsome—don't you think so?"

"Very. How strangely alike he and Mr. Norton are!"

"At first sight, yes; but only at first sight, I think. Mr. Norton has much the more brilliant colouring, while Captain Norman is a much more strongly-built man."

"Fine fellows both," said Victor, in a tone of admiration; "well knit, well proportioned. I hardly know which I think the finer-looking man of the two."

"I always admire dark men," said Élise; "fair men are so insipid, as a rule." Then she pretended to notice how fair was Victor for the first time. "How rude of me!" she added. "I see now that you are a fair man. However, you must forgive me; I am such a dreadful hand at paying compliments. I always blurt out just what I think, you know. At any rate, I do not think you insipid."

Victor was charmed. He honestly liked a woman who had a soul above humbug; a woman who spoke her mind openly and boldly. Such a woman, doubtless, was Miss Desmoulines.

His attention, however, was at the moment diverted to Captain Norman, who had choked over his wine. Captain Norman had heard Élise's praise of dark manly beauty. He also remembered Élise's remarks on her preference for fair men made to Planty Broom at the Coddesley dinner-party. Captain Norman's sense of humour had been too much for him. Hence the choke.

Mrs. Astor had a bad time of it at Miss Priscilla's. In the excitement of London life, its constant bustle, and hurry, and confusion, she had not had much time for thought of any kind, certainly not for probing her own affections. But latterly, since she had given way to the scheme of chaperoning Élise at Olton Priors, while the latter prosecuted her designs on Plantagenet Broom, Mrs. Astor had had nothing on earth to do but to think, to probe her own heart, and, lastly, to find out that she really cared for Conrad Norton more than she thought she ever could have cared for any man again.

Her sister's mere suggestion that Lady Margate had once been beloved by Conrad had been sufficient to cause a throb of jealousy in Mrs. Astor's breast. When she had understood that Conrad meant to marry Genista Broom, if he could get her, she had suffered much, though the very knowledge that her rival would be married solely for her money was some consolation; but what Mrs. Astor discovered for herself at Miss Priscilla's was the cruellest stab of all.

Conrad had taken Eva Ross in to dinner. The eyes of love are sharp ; Mrs. Astor very soon saw that Eva's beauty had made an impression on Conrad's nature, which was gathering intensity with every moment he spent in the girl's society. In the midst of his brightest sallies, when his brilliant conversation was most telling, Mrs. Astor noticed the almost gloomy passion that burnt ever and anon in Conrad's eyes as he looked at Eva Ross. To lose him to a woman whom he would hate was one thing ; but that he should marry a woman whom he could love in preference to herself was another. Mrs. Astor did not enjoy herself at the Manor House.

She had given both Conrad and Élise credit for a heartlessness they did not possess. She considered her sister and her friend to be very bad people—much worse, indeed, than herself—and, as is the way with shallow persons, she had imagined that the worse people are in a moral point of view, the less they share ordinary human passions—the less human they are altogether.

Mrs. Astor's error was a very common one. The possession of vices is no safeguard against other weaknesses. The warping of the moral qualities is no preventive to the poison of Love's arrows. The human fiend is human still; only part of the worst man's nature is diseased.

Élise had loved not at all; Conrad too often. The result with the former would be a reaction that might grow to frenzied passion when love was once aroused. The result with the latter a gross sensuality that could brook no barriers to its gratification.

But Mrs. Astor was a shallow woman in all respects. She was vain, and crafty, and designing; but life was viewed by her in altogether a superficial manner. She had loved, but not so as to hurt herself much ; she had sinned, but the sin had not brought that repentance, or even contrition, which a nobler nature, or even a worse one, might have felt. Still, it was gall and wormwood to her that Conrad should love another woman before her very eyes.

After dinner, Conrad never relaxed in his devoted attentions to Miss Ross. Captain Norman was too much of a gentleman to cut in where opportunity was wanting. Eva thought he was out of spirits because Diana was not present. That Lord Margate's brother should prefer her to Diana Trevor had not entered her head; though in her heart of hearts there was no man who could be compared to Captain Norman.

George Warre made the most of his opportunity with Camilla Howard. She was too proud a girl to angle for any man ; but if she had doubted before as to who had her heart in his keeping, she no longer doubted after this eventful evening at the Manor House.

She had said that she found gentlemen insipid. George Warre was not a gentleman, and he certainly was not insipid. The man's bold wooing was delightful to her. He showed her by every glance of his bold brown eyes what passion lay concealed behind them. His very voice was full of his love. Camilla's vigorous nature bounded to meet his. After to-night, the shape of the young Lanes assumed the proportions of rag dolls more vividly than ever in Camilla Howard's eyes.

Penelope saw and wondered. To her George Warre was but an incarnation of brute strength. She admitted that he was a fine young fellow, broad-shouldered, muscular, and vigorous. But the man was rough and coarse, and his conversation and dress were horsy and fast; at least, so thought Penelope—but then Penelope was not in love with George Warre.

Mr. Pericles Bone was very attentive to Penelope. Mr. Bone was aware that his being an unmarried man was a disadvantage to him in his profession. A good many families put up with the aged imbecilities of Dr. Grain simply because they preferred having a married man to attend their families.

Mr. Bone had been heard to say that when he married he must have a "sound" woman with a little money. Penelope Howard was very "sound," and had a good deal of money. Altogether, without being what is termed "in love," Mr. Pericles Bone was attracted to the Howard money and the Howard "soundness." Perhaps he would have preferred Camilla; but he was quite keen enough to see that Camilla would not have him.

A good many things were settled at Miss Priscilla's that evening, and a good many hearts and purposes were unsettled. It is certain, at any rate, that Élise had fallen in love with Victor Ross, while still adhering to her determination to get engaged to Planty Broom; and that Conrad Norton had lost such heart as he possessed to Eva, which made Genista Broom even more distasteful to him than before. Also Mrs. Astor began to be jealous and unhappy. She had not even any one to flirt with, and she found Olton Priors very dull.

Miss Desmoulines had made Victor promise to bring her some carnations the following morning on his way to the timber-yard. She also took to sketching, and thought the view she should commence with was one of the river from Ross's wharf. Could he lend her a chair, and provide her with a tumbler of water, etc., if she carried out her intention? Yes, of course he could!

So the thin end of the wedge was inserted, and Victor was drawn, inch by inch, into the net of this siren's weaving, all because Élise had been so enthusiastic in her praises of Diana Trevor.

CHAPTER XXI.

N the following day Captain Norman received a telegram from Lady Margate, asking him to come to London immediately, as Lord Margate was much worse. Of course he went there and then.

When, on the preceding evening, he had noticed Conrad Norton's attention to Eva Ross, he had made up his mind to speak to Eva forthwith, and give her clearly to understand how dear she was to him; but so urgent a telegram as Lady Margate's admitted of no delay, so the word was not spoken.

Eva, like every one else, believed that Captain Norman would return to propose to Diana Trevor. The match would be very suitable. The " county " had quite expected such a marriage to come off, and the " county " was disposed to take great credit to itself for its sagacity.

It was with a sigh, however, that Eva Ross had admitted to herself the extreme suitability of such an arrangement. Diana was now her closest friend; yet Diana did not show in any way that she cared for the frequent visits Captain Norman had paid at the Priory, to play pyramids with Mr. Trevor. Diana made no confidences to Eva. Diana's treatment of Captain Norman was cavalier to a degree. Eva would almost have thought Diana was indifferent to the handsome young fellow; but every one said

it was Diana's way, and every one also said
that the thing was as good as settled—Diana
would one day be Countess of Margate.

There was one thing, however, which
nettled Eva Ross greatly. Eva, like Victor,
was very truthful and honest, and she
believed what other people said implicitly,
if those people were in her opinion trust-
worthy in character generally. Diana always
spoke slightingly of Victor to Eva—always
praised the qualities Victor did not possess;
raved about manner and wit, and style and
accomplishments, in none of which Victor
shone; and expressed herself in a disparag-
ing way about such qualities as Victor undoubtedly possessed.

When Captain Norman was present, Diana
kept up a perpetual volley of "chaff" and
banter; but when Victor came, Diana became suddenly silent, and seemed to resent
any effort to draw her out or amuse her.

All this hurt Eva very much. She was afraid Victor must distress Diana's sensitive ness by his blunt ways; yet she did not like to blame Victor, even to herself.

On the day following Miss Priscilla's dinner-party, Diana Trevor walked over to Black Rock to lunch with Eva Ross, and have a gossip about the party.

It was a sultry July day; Diana, accompanied by Fido the spaniel, who was her constant friend and companion, arrived at Black Rock very hot and tired.

"I cannot think why Miss Priscilla left me out," was almost the first remark she made, after she sat down to luncheon. "It was so unlike her to have a lot of young people together without asking me."

"I think the dinner was originally intended to bring George Warre within the pale of civilisation," said Eva, "and I fancy

Miss Priscilla was a little nervous as to his behaviour in society."

" He wouldn't have eaten me instead of beef or mutton, I suppose," said Diana pertly ; " though there is something of the ogre about him certainly, now I come to think of him."

" Now, Diana, I won't hear George Warre abused. He is one of the best of men—a good, honest, brave soul as ever lived. Victor loves him almost as a brother."

" Yes ! I suppose he is the sort of young giant who would find favour with your brother. Let me see—what is the right expression to use ? Oh ! I know ! ' not an ounce of flesh to spare, all bone and muscle, as clean built a young fellow as ever entered the ring ;' that is what Mr. Victor Ross always says, if one but mentions the name of George Warre ;" and Diana laughed a little provoking flippant laugh.

Eva was hurt.

"I cannot see why you should always make fun of Victor," she said in a wounded tone. "It is not his fault that he has been brought up among men who place an exaggerated value on personal strength. Victor always says what he can in favour of his friends. Why should he not praise George Warre's muscular strength?"

"I wonder what Mr. Victor Ross finds to say in favour of me?" retorted Diana; "does he consider me clean built? Does he think I could train a bit finer? There! feel my biceps! Eva," and the wild girl clenched her little fist and bent her arm as she had seen young fellows do in school-boy's rivalry, before she came to Olton Priors.

But Eva was rather shocked.

"My dear Diana," she said gravely, "I wish you would not go off in such a wild

way. Of course Victor says everything that
is nice and kind of you."

"Oh! now does he really? That is uncommonly good of him. I am glad I have
earned your brother's good opinion, Eva."

Eva looked up, surprised at Diana's
tone. There was a ring of pride in it
that jarred upon Eva's nerves. But Eva
was not a girl of keen sensibilities, and she
had never dreamed how matters really stood
between Victor and Diana.

"Well! what are the nice and kind things
your brother says of me?" said Diana, with
persistent flippancy.

"He thinks you amiable, Diana."

"Anything else?"

"And intelligent," added Eva.

Diana bounced off her seat like an exas-
perated sparrow from its twig. She rushed
up to the glass over the mantelpiece, and
bowed mockingly to her image.

"Amiable and intelligent," she said, "how truly flattering! amiable and intelligent! Upon my word, Eva, your brother does me too much honour, but he does not show much discernment of character; I am not amiable, certainly, and I thought Fido was what would be called intelligent. Come here, Fido, do you think I am amiable and—and intelligent?"

Fido put his paws on Diana, and poked his nose into her hand, wagging his tail the while, in affirmation of anything he might be intended to affirm.

Suddenly Diana threw herself into her seat again. The spirit of mischief danced in her eyes.

"Tell me all about Captain Norman, Eva. How did he look? What did he say? Oh! what a darling that man is, is he not?"

"I cannot understand your ways, Diana. How wildly you talk."

"Well! but he is a darling, isn't he now? Come, confess."

"I don't know what you mean, Diana," said Eva, getting very red and uncomfortable. "I am not in the habit of calling any young men my darlings. Captain Norman was there, looking much as usual, but he seemed out of spirits, and did not say more than 'how d'ye do' to me the whole evening."

"What!" exclaimed Diana, in so sharp a tone that Fido dropped his bone in dismay.

"Captain Norman was doubtless upset about his brother," continued Eva; "and I suppose he was—was vexed at finding that he had been brought there on false pretences."

Eva said this with a little laugh, which was meant to be sly; but Diana showed no spark of that "intelligence" with which she was supposed to be gifted.

" How on false pretences ?" said Diana.

" Well, of course he came to meet some one, who was not there."

"The more fool he ! but I want to know who was expected that was not there."

" Why ! you, of course ! Whom else do you suppose he wanted to see ?"

Diana opened her dark eyes very wide, in speechless amazement. Was it really possible that Eva Ross was so simple, so modest, so innocent as not to know that Captain Norman was head over ears in love with her ? Yet there was not a blush on her cheek, or a tremor in her voice, when she spoke of him !

Diana put both her elbows on the table, and leaned her face on her upturned palms. In this attitude she regarded Eva with much serious curiosity for some moments. Then she whistled. She had heard Victor say it was unladylike for a girl to whistle, and she had immediately practised in private for Victor's benefit in public. This was one of Diana's little ways.

Eva had been taught not to put her elbows on the table, not to stare hard at people, and not to whistle; but Diana was not like other people. Diana was very nice, but she was certainly odd.

"My dear," said Diana.

"Well!"

"You are amiable, there is no doubt of that."

"I am glad you think so."

"But not intelligent! no! certainly not intelligent."

Then Diana burst out into a paroxysm of laughter, and hugged Fido, to the latter's huge delight, till she had not another laugh in her.

Eva looked on gravely. She was beginning to feel rather offended.

· "I see no joke," she said rather shortly. "Pray enlighten me. I should like to laugh too if I knew what to laugh at."

For answer Diana came round the table and put a little hand on each side of Eva's fair bright face, and gazed down into her eyes, almost as Captain Norman might have longed to do. Then she kissed Eva, and thought how like Victor she was; but she kept this thought to herself.

"And now tell me more about Captain Norman, Eva," she said as she sat down again; "you don't know how I doat on that man."

"I won't talk to you at all, Diana, if you speak in such an unbecoming manner; doat on him indeed, why! even if you were engaged to him, you ought not to use such an expression."

"I dare say not, dear, but then you see I

am not engaged to him, and, what is more, I never mean to be."

" Diana !"

" Never mean to be, never mean to be, never mean to be !" repeated Diana, nodding her little head demurely from the opposite side of the table.

" Why ! every one supposes that you are as good as engaged to him already."

" Then every one had best suppose something else as soon as every one likes."

" But, Diana, people will say you have behaved shamefully, after all the attention he has paid you."

" People may say what they please, my dear Eva ; Captain Norman is nothing to me, nor I to him.   If I were not useful to him, he would rather dislike me than otherwise."

" Then why has he been to the Priory day after day for the last fortnight or more ?" asked Eva innocently.

" I suppose it was to play pyramids with papa," answered Diana mischievously.

Eva shook her head sagely.

" A man does not care to play pyramids day after day for three weeks with a two-mile walk at each end of the game," she said.

Diana did not think so either, but she did not feel called upon to make Captain Norman's proposal for him, so she abruptly changed the subject.

" What do you think of these new people at 'The Willows,' Eva, Mrs. Astor and Miss Desmoulines, and that Adonis, Mr. Conrad Norton ?"

" I have hardly spoken to either of the ladies. Victor tells me that Miss Desmoulines is charming, and that she raves about you."

" She does not even know me."

" About your beauty, and manner, and style, and all that sort of thing."

"I am sorry I cannot return the compliment. I may wrong Miss Desmoulines, but
she does not give me the impression of being
a lady. How did you get on with Mr.
Norton ?"

"He took me in to dinner. I think him
quite delightful."

"As delightful as Captain Norman ?"

"One cannot compare the two men."

"Why not ? They are very much alike."

"In outline only ; Mr. Norton is far the
handsomer, Captain Norman much the better
looking."

"What do you mean by that ?"

"Mr. Norton is one of the most beautiful
creatures I ever saw. He is so sleek and
velvety, I should like to stroke him."

"Just like a superb tiger," suggested
Diana.

"Just so ; I am not usually enthusiastic
about beauty, but I think I never saw any

human being quite so beautiful as Mr. Norton."

"He looks very clean," said Diana sneeringly.

"He has a very good figure," continued Eva, not heeding the sneer, "at least Victor says so, and Victor is a good judge of a man's build."

"So one would suppose," interrupted Diana again. "When your brother gets on that theme, he is as good as a treatise on the anatomy of the ancient Greeks."

"I presume you do not like Mr. Norton, Diana," said Eva, ignoring as usual her friend's depreciatory remarks about her brother.

"No! I do not! that is a fact. I do not act on matured judgment like you and your brother, Eva; I am an impulsive, prejudiced, happy-go-lucky little sinner, who takes strong likes and dislikes at first sight. Sometimes

I repent in the middle, but I come back at last to my first impressions. Mr. Norton is distasteful to me, I cannot tell why. He is beautiful beyond words, I quite admit that. He combines the manliness of the one sex with the softness of the other. This combination makes him especially dangerous, either as friend or lover. The man's voice is delicious, his manner is in itself an implied caress, yet I believe he is a perfect fiend!"

"It is positively wicked of you to say such things, Diana. You own you know nothing of Mr. Norton; you have not exchanged a dozen sentences with him in your life, and yet you presume to judge him."

"I can forgive most sins and some vices in a man," said Diana, "but not hypocrisy, or cruelty, or ingratitude. In Mr. Norton I believe I see these three qualities in their ripest perfection. Look at his eyes!"

" They look you straight in the face," said Eva.

" They do, but they are masked for all that. No thorough-bred villain is weak enough to have a shifting gaze. That bold, honest look is part of the stock-in-trade of an accomplished rascal. Mr. Norton's eyes are so black that you can see no expression in them. To guess at his thoughts you must watch his mouth. His command over that feature is not so well trained. His lips are thin; their expression is cruel and cynical to the last degree."

" I confess I have not watched him so closely as you appear to have done," said Eva, smiling. " George Warre is enthusiastic about him, and Victor seems to like him too."

" Talk of the devil !" exclaimed Diana, starting up; " I mean Mr. Norton, not his companion. Look ! there are your brother and the gentleman in question coming up the garden walk."

The words were hardly spoken before the two young men entered the room.

CHAPTER XXII.

A RASH PROPOSAL.

" I HAVE come to be introduced to the beauties of your garden, Miss Ross," said Conrad as he entered. " Your brother has been showing me some lovely scenery on the road, a view of the Priory, too, Miss Trevor, that is quite enchanting."

Diana gave him a discouraging little bow. She had not offered to shake hands with him, and had retired into the window-sill. Eva knew that when Victor was present, Diana would not say a word. Feeling unwilling to make conversation for the quartette, she at once proposed to show Mr. Norton the gardens. She walked on ahead with Conrad, while Diana and Victor followed.

" I thought I had heard that Mr. Norton was going to stay at Buncombe," said Diana, as she and Victor strolled up the gardens to the Wilderness.

" So he is to-morrow," answered Victor, " I am very sorry for it. George Warre will miss him terribly, and I confess I should have liked to see more of him."

" What is to prevent you ?"

" I do not know the Buncombe people, with the exception of the son and heir, whom I cannot endure."

" Nor I."

" I thought you had got over your first impressions about him."

" I have returned to them. It is my fate to do so. First impressions with me are nearly always correct."

" I am glad to hear you say that."

" Why ?"

" Do you remember the day I was introduced to you ?"

Diana flushed crimson and looked away across the valley.

"Yes, quite well," she said in a low tone, " but what of that ?"

" I gave you some myrtles just here. I cut them from this bush."

"Well! what has that to do with first impressions ?"

" Only that it set me thinking, and hoping that perhaps some day you might return to a kinder impression of me than you have had of late."

" There has never been any impression to return to. I have thought the same of you throughout, from the first time I saw you."

" Then you have veiled your thoughts very skilfully."

" What do you mean ?"

" That your impression of me before you saw Captain Norman was more favourable than it is now," said the young man moodily.

Diana looked up in genuine surprise. " How blind men are !" thought she to herself. " What is Captain Norman to me ?" she answered.

" That is just what I want to know," said Victor.

" What right have you to know anything about it ?" said Diana, firing up.

" What, indeed ?" said Victor with a sigh. He stood irresolute a moment, looking out over Black Tor, and the gurgling stream that beat against the granite boulder at their feet.

"You are not engaged to Captain Norman, Miss Trevor?"

"Certainly not; neither of us care a rush about one another."

"But all the neighbourhood says so."

"It is a free country; the neighbourhood might say I was engaged to Mr. Pericles Bone, if it chose, and with quite as much reason."

Victor's bright blue eyes flashed down on her with a gleam of hope. "I dare say I am a fool," said he, "but after all, it is, as you say, a free country; speech is the common right of all."

Diana laughed uneasily. She looked up at him, and found his blue eyes fastened on her with, oh! such a look of love.

"I love you with all my heart and soul, Diana."

"And I you, Victor."

He lifted her slender form from the ground, and strained her to his breast.

"My love! my love!" she whispered as she nestled her face close in his yellow beard. "Have you not known how I loved you all along?"

"I hardly dared hope," said he, "I am but a plain timber-merchant, and you are a mate fit for princes."

"And I have chosen my own king. The whole world contains nothing for me but you, my own, own love."

END OF VOL. II.

BILLING AND SONS, PRINTERS, GUILDFORD, SURREY.

www.ingramcontent.com/pod-product-compliance
Lightning Source LLC
Chambersburg PA
CBHW020844020726
47497CB00005B/1252